P9-CLC-245

WHO IN THE WORLD IS
CARMEN
SANDIEGO?™

Copyright © 2019 by HMH IP Company Unlimited Company.
Carmen Sandiego and associated logos and design are trademarks of HMH
IP Company Unlimited Company.

All rights reserved. For information about permission to reproduce selections
from this book, write to trade.permissions@hmhco.com or to Permissions,
Houghton Mifflin Harcourt Publishing Company, 3 Park Avenue, 19th
Floor, New York, New York 10016.

hmhco.com

The text was set in Adobe Garamond Pro.

Library of Congress Cataloging-in-Publication Data
Names: Tinker, Rebecca, adapter. | Capizzi, Duane, screenwriter.
Title: Who in the world is Carmen Sandiego? / adaptation by Rebecca Tinker ;
based on the teleplay by Duane Capizzi ; with a foreword by Gina Rodriguez.
Description: Boston ; New York : Houghton Mifflin Harcourt, [2019] |
Series: Carmen Sandiego Identifiers: LCCN 2018020063 |
ISBN 9781328495297 (paper over board) Subjects: | BISAC: JUVENILE
FICTION / Media Tie - In. | JUVENILE FICTION / Action & Adventure /
General. | JUVENILE FICTION / Law & Crime.
Classification: LCC PZ7.1.T57 Wh 2019 |
DDC [Fic]—dc23
LC record available at https://lccn.loc.gov/2018020063

Printed in the United States of America
DOC 10 9 8 7 6 5 4 3 2 1
4500739475

WHO IN THE WORLD IS
CARMEN SANDIEGO?™

Adaptation by Rebecca Tinker
Based on the teleplay by Duane Capizzi

With a foreword
by Gina Rodriguez

HOUGHTON MIFFLIN HARCOURT

BOSTON NEW YORK

FOREWORD

By Gina Rodriguez

CARMEN SANDIEGO WAS ALWAYS A HERO TO ME. THAT may sound odd, since for so long there was little we really knew about her other than that she was a master thief. And I certainly didn't want to be a thief.

My sisters and I grew up with *Where in the World Is Carmen Sandiego?* We chased her across the globe through a computer game and a TV game show. It's true, we didn't really know who she was or why she was doing the things she did. But here's what I did know: Carmen Sandiego was traveling—she was getting out in the world, seeing all kinds of places and exploring different cultures. I idolized those things about her. The rest of Carmen's story was a mystery, but I could fill that in with my imagination. I wanted to see the world and be a sponge of knowledge, soaking it all up, just like Carmen Sandiego.

But now we don't have to imagine a story for Carmen anymore. After all those years of asking "Where in the world is Carmen Sandiego?," it's time to turn our attention to an even more important question: *Who* in the world is Carmen Sandiego? What is her backstory? Where does she come from? Why does she steal? And how did she get to be so good at it?

At her core, Carmen is a strong, humble, and brave woman who is trying to heal the pain of her past, and in doing so, she is helping so many around her. I don't think anyone sets out to be a hero or a role model. I don't think that's how you become those things. But when you set out to follow your dreams—when you set goals and go after them with hard work and persistence and faith and integrity—then you start creating a path that others will want to follow because of the light that you shine. If you set out to be the best version of yourself, there's no way you can go wrong. And that's what Carmen does. It takes some trial and error. Of course, there are bumps along the way. But Carmen shows us that if you allow failure and rejection to exist, and know that they are an inevitable part of life, they will only make you stronger on your journey to success.

As the voice of Carmen, I have the opportunity to portray the type of fearless and empowered woman that I want to be. Carmen stands up for what she believes in. She gives opportunity to those who have none, and that's why she is a role model to me. That is what I want to do with my life: create opportunity where I see there is none, sharing my blessings and giving my blessings away so that I can create room for more and give more to others.

I feel so lucky to be a part of the Carmen Sandiego world. When I was approached for this role, I actually started crying! I just couldn't believe that I was getting to do the voice of Carmen Sandiego. I knew that one of my childhood idols, Rita Moreno, had been the voice of Carmen in a previous iteration, and this felt like the passing of the torch. I had never done a project that my family was familiar with before, and it was so much fun to be able to tell them that I would be the next Carmen. Finally, everybody knew this character that I was taking on, and they couldn't believe I was being blessed with this honor. I know how vital it was when I was younger to see myself represented on screen. I hope that Carmen Sandiego can be a reflection of courage and strength and feminism today the way I imagined her to be when I was a kid. When you follow your dreams, you give others the allowance to follow theirs. I have been working so hard to prepare myself and to create a foundation of self-love and self-care so that I can go out and accomplish my dreams and be fearless in doing so. Just like Carmen.

 GINA RODRIGUEZ, born and raised in Chicago, currently lives in Los Angeles and is a graduate of New York University's Tisch School of the Arts. Gina can be seen playing the title role on the CW series *Jane the Virgin,* for which she won the Golden Globe for Best Actress in a Television Series–Musical or Comedy in 2015. Her voice can be heard as Carmen Sandiego in the Netflix animated series. In addition to acting, Rodriguez is a leader in supporting inclusion and the empowerment of women. This passion led her to create her production company, I Can and I Will Productions, with a mission to create art that tells stories from the traditionally unseen and unheard. She also established the We Will Foundation with her family, which is designed to focus on arts education and scholarship funding for the less fortunate, with the aim of championing and lifting up young women and men.

CHAPTER 1

THE SUN WAS ABOUT TO SET IN THE HISTORIC CITY of Poitiers, France. The medieval cathedrals were aglow with the golden light of dusk as residents made their way home across cobblestone streets.

Yet there was one Poitiers resident who had no intention of going home that night.

In a sleek black car parked in the city square, Inspector Chase Devineaux clenched the steering wheel, his knuckles turning a pale shade of white.

For the past two days, ever since the infamous globetrotting thief known as Carmen Sandiego was rumored to have arrived in his city, the French Interpol officer had dedicated every waking moment to organizing her capture. Everyone was after Carmen Sandiego, and she had managed to dodge agencies and officers all over the world. Chase had not slept; he had barely eaten — for he knew that this could be his only chance to make an arrest. Finally, the super thief was in his jurisdiction, and he would not let this opportunity go to waste. *I will catch her if it is the last thing I do,* Chase thought.

He turned to Julia Argent, sitting in the passenger seat next to him. She was studiously scrolling through data on her tablet. Julia was a newly recruited Interpol officer with sleek black hair that she kept very short and round glasses that magnified her already large brown eyes. She was half Chinese and half British, and she had a knack for things like languages and history. But what she was *really* good at was solving problems using logic. Chase had already come to realize in just a few days of working with her that what Julia lacked in experience, she made up for in intellect. And he would never admit it, but that intimidated him.

Julia adjusted her glasses and looked closely at her screen as she scrolled through a series of blurred images. The images all showed the same woman in different exotic locations across the globe. In one, she was leaving a bank in Hong Kong. In another, she was boarding a train in Norway. In every photograph, the mysterious woman wore the same vibrant red trench coat and matching fedora tilted at a perfect angle on her head. But her face was always covered, as though she knew the exact moment to look away and keep her features hidden.

"In the last few weeks alone, this *Carmen Sandiego* has stolen millions from a Swiss bank, a high-end art gallery in Cairo, and a Shanghai amusement park!" Chase exclaimed as he tightened his grip on the steering wheel even more.

Julia nodded, her eyes still on the data in front of her. "We've yet to find any pattern. Don't you find it strange, sir, that she seems to announce her crimes by making public appearances beforehand? Like the café sighting here in Poitiers earlier today?"

Chase grumbled under his breath. Those same questions had been bothering him for weeks now. Why would a thief draw attention to herself by leaving clues and wearing such bold colors? Was stealing just a game to Carmen Sandiego? *Catch me if you can!*

He brushed away the thought with a wave of his hand. "It does not matter," he said firmly. "She is in my city now, Ms. Argent, and I will be the one to capture her!"

Julia's attention was suddenly drawn toward the sight of a red blur as a figure darted across the street in front of their car. Julia's breath caught in her chest. *Could it be?*

Chase Devineaux continued, not seeing the red figure directly ahead of him. "You are new to the force, so you are to sit back, watch me work, and learn how to catch a thief!"

Julia bolted upright and hurriedly pointed in the direction of the woman. "Sir! She's right there!"

Annoyed at the interruption, Chase slowly turned to follow the direction of Julia's finger with a frustrated sigh. *New officers are too excitable these days,* he thought.

Then Chase caught sight of a red fedora across the street. His eyes went wide. It was the woman in red!

"*La Femme Rouge!*" Chase shouted. Carmen Sandiego fired a grapnel overhead and was gracefully pulled skyward toward the rooftops. She had been right in front of him — and now she was getting away!

ON AN ORANGE-TILED ROOFTOP, CARMEN SANDIEGO looked across the Poitiers skyline and stopped to take in the incredible view. In the distance, she could see the towers of Cathédrale Saint-Pierre lit up by the sun's dimming rays. Her long brown hair fell in waves from under her red fedora. She tilted the hat up and away from her eyes and sighed deeply at the sight.

She never tired of the magnificent sights to be found in new and exciting places around the world. Even now, when she knew time was of the essence, she couldn't help but take a moment to appreciate how beautiful France was.

"You might want to save the sightseeing for after the job," came the voice of a young teenage boy in her ear.

Carmen touched the earring that doubled as a communication device and smiled wryly. "Glad you could join me, Player."

"I wouldn't miss a night out with you for the world, Red," he responded.

Player was Carmen Sandiego's confidante and, one could say, her very best friend, even though they had never actually met face-to-face. Player also had incredible computer-hacking abilities that far surpassed his years. Carmen realized that she had come to rely on the computer whiz while she was out in the field.

"The next stop on your sightseeing tour of Poitiers should be . . . fifty yards dead ahead," Player instructed.

Carmen darted forward across the rooftops, her boots clicking like castanets across the tiles. The steep angles of the roofs posed no difficulty for her as she jumped from one building to another.

Soon enough, she reached her destination. It was a French chateau penthouse. Hanging vines grew along the sides of the building, reaching down to a balcony where Carmen spied a set of large glass doors. *But I'm not going in through the door,* she thought with a slight smile.

With one smooth motion, Carmen made a final leap to the penthouse roof and scanned the area until she found what she was looking for — a skylight window. Kneeling down, Carmen examined a security-alarm box connected to the side of it. If she tried to open the window without disabling the alarm first, every police officer in France would be after her in an instant.

Without missing a beat, Carmen took out a tube of lipstick from her coat pocket and twisted the bottom. But Carmen was not one for doing her makeup on the job. She was much more interested in the high-tech port that extended from the lipstick tube. She slid it into the side of the alarm box with a *click*. "Cosmetic *and* electric," Carmen said with a smile. "Do you think you can open this for me, Player?"

"Matching frequencies . . . decrypting the security codes . . ." he mumbled. Carmen could hear Player typing rapidly from where he lived in Ontario, Canada. While she had never seen his computer-hacking station, she had no doubt he had multiple monitors and all the latest in high-tech computer technology. "And you're in! Alarm system disabled."

The light on the security box changed from red to green, and Carmen slid the skylight window open. *Too easy,* she thought. It was always more fun when she was able to put her skills to the test.

"It could be a trap," Player cautioned.

"Let's find out."

Carmen pulled her grappling hook out of her trench coat. Gadgets of all shapes and sizes lined the inside of her fashionable red coat, always within arm's reach.

She secured the grappling hook to the edge of the skylight and began lowering herself into the chateau.

Carmen soon found herself in a thief's paradise. She was surrounded by ornate suits of armor, priceless tapestries, and delicate porcelain vases lining the mantels. She reached the floor, and as she stepped down—

Click!

Suddenly, a hidden panel opened in the wall, and out fired a fleet of crossbow bolts. The sharp metal arrows were coming straight at her, deadly and fast. There was no time to lose! Carmen grabbed a shield from a nearby suit of armor and raised it to protect herself. With dull thuds, the arrows buried themselves in the shield.

Carmen winced at the sight of the medieval shield now peppered with arrows. With a twinge of guilt for damaging a priceless antique, she set the shield aside and made her way through the chateau.

Perhaps other people would have been on edge after being shot at with arrows, but for Carmen Sandiego, it was just another Tuesday.

Carmen looked around the vast living area, and her eyes settled on a bookshelf that reached all the way from the floor to the ceiling. "Isn't this where the vault should be?" Carmen asked as she began running her hand along the shelves.

"According to the blueprints, yes," Player agreed. Carmen rapped her hand on the shelf, and a hollow echo sounded back. She quickly scanned the wall, knowing that the door had to be there somewhere. Carmen reached up and pulled down on a bronze candlestick that was attached to the wall. *Bingo!* She grinned as the bookshelf swung open to reveal a huge metal door.

The vault door was securely locked with an electronic keypad, so Carmen pulled another gadget from the inside of her coat. This one was her own small yet sleek keypad. With the press of a button, numbers began to flash on the keypad's screen, one after another, as it searched for the combination that would open the vault. After a moment, a sequence of numbers locked in place on the screen. *Open sesame,* thought Carmen as the vault door swung open. She stepped inside.

The vault was a massive, cave-like room. Glittering jewels and ancient antiques lined the walls. They must have been worth a small fortune. The real prize, however, rested in the middle of the room on a glass pedestal. Carmen walked toward it, her excitement rising.

Directly in front of her was a blue gemstone the size of a football. It was known to collectors and archaeologists as the famed Eye of Vishnu. It was an incredible sight to behold, and it was one that Carmen had seen once before, a long time ago.

But Carmen had no time to reminisce about the past. She quickly approached the Eye of Vishnu, reaching out to take it from the pedestal. Just then, something in the corner of the room caught her eye.

She gasped — *It couldn't be!*

"Red? What's wrong?"

Carmen swallowed, trying to process what she was seeing. "I'm staring at something I thought I'd never, ever set eyes on again," she told Player, her voice raw with emotion.

"Is what you're staring at more valuable than *the Eye of Vishnu?* You know, the gemstone that's as big as my head?" Player asked, confused about what could have possibly distracted Carmen from her mission.

Before Carmen could answer Player's question, there was a loud pounding at the penthouse door.

"Interpol! Open this door!"

Carmen whirled around. A smile played at the corner of her mouth. Now, *this* was just the sort of challenge she liked.

INSPECTOR CHASE DEVINEAUX KNEW HIS WINDOW OF opportunity for catching Carmen Sandiego was small. "Open up! This is Interpol!" he yelled again, and slammed his whole body into the door, breaking it open.

He ran into the vault just in time to see the red-coated Carmen Sandiego swinging a black satchel over her shoulder, a round object stored inside it. Chase's cheeks reddened with anger. "Stop! Thief!"

He lunged at her, but Carmen had pulled a medieval tapestry down from the wall and was now waving it like a Spanish matador facing a bull. She skillfully tossed the fabric wall hanging around him, and Chase found himself in complete darkness. He struggled to pull it off. Finally, Chase threw the tapestry aside, sputtering.

"Inspector Chase Devineaux, huh?" Carmen Sandiego asked with a wry smile.

Chase stared at her, dumbfounded. *How does she know my name?* he wondered. He reached for his pockets and gasped as he found them empty.

Carmen Sandiego held up his badge and tossed it back to him. His jaw dropped. *How did she get that?*

"Let's see what's in a name, Chase," she said. Before the inspector could formulate a response, Carmen fired her grappling hook overhead and disappeared through the skylight window.

Chase glanced around. Beyond a set of large windows, he could see a fire escape—it had to lead to the roof! He pushed open the window, raced up the fire escape, and jumped onto the roof. He could feel every second tick by as he saw Carmen Sandiego sprinting nimbly across the

French rooftops. "I ordered you to stop!" Chase called after her, struggling to keep up.

To his surprise, Carmen did stop. She turned around. "You didn't say for how long," Carmen teased, and in an instant, she was off running again.

Across the rooftops they ran until Chase saw that Carmen was headed straight for the edge of a tall building, with nowhere left to run or jump. *I've got her now,* he thought triumphantly, and began to imagine the glory he would receive as the inspector who finally captured the world's most elusive thief.

Carmen reached the roof's edge and turned to face Chase Devineaux. He smiled. This was it. He had her right where he wanted her, and she had nowhere to go. But to his surprise, she simply waved.

"*Au revoir,*" Carmen said, and she stepped off the roof.

Chase stared in disbelief as red hang-glider wings extended from a backpack strapped to Carmen's back. She soared up and over the streets of Poitiers with grace and ease. "Impossible!" he exclaimed.

As he watched her make her escape, he realized a moment too late that he was standing too close to the roof's edge. Suddenly, his foot began to slip. Chase lost his balance and catapulted down toward the road below.

CRASH!

He fell right onto the front of his own car that was

still parked below. With a groan, he looked through the cracked windshield to see a shocked Julia Argent gazing up at him from the passenger seat.

"Inspector! Are you all right?"

"Never mind that!" Chase pointed skyward to where Carmen Sandiego was gliding, a bright flash of red against the twilight sky. "I must follow her! Now!"

Chase threw open the door to the car, ignoring the cracked windshield. Julia leaned forward, her eyes trained on the woman in the sky. "She must land sometime . . ." Julia thought aloud.

Realization suddenly dawned on Chase. "She is heading for the train station! Ms. Argent, go to the crime scene and figure out what was stolen. I will catch her before she makes her escape!" Julia jumped out of the car, and Chase slammed his foot on the gas pedal.

The car screeched through the narrow streets of Poitiers. As he neared the train station, Chase looked up to see Carmen Sandiego soar down for an elegant landing, disappearing behind the station building. Despite himself, Chase couldn't help but admire—just for a moment—the grace with which this mysterious woman seemed to operate.

His foot still firmly on the gas pedal, Chase sped the car up alongside the station just in time to see the train pulling away. He turned his car toward the train tracks, and with a twist of the steering wheel, the car lurched up next to the tracks. "I am *not* letting her get away!"

CARMEN MADE HER WAY THROUGH THE TRAIN CAR UNTIL she located her compartment, then stepped in and shut the door behind her.

In an impossibly fast move, Carmen had changed from her red trench coat and fedora into jeans and a red hoodie. It was a skill she had learned a long time ago in an unusual class at an even more unusual school, and it served her well in times like these. Getaways were most successful when you blended in with the crowd, she thought. The plush velvet seats in the train car and the passing French scenery out the window were welcome sights. "First class? Nice!" Carmen said with a smile as she sat down.

"You've earned it," Player responded. Carmen couldn't argue with that. It had certainly been a successful job.

She picked up her black satchel. It was heavy with the weight of the stolen object.

From where he was on the other side of the world, Player was beginning to wonder whether Carmen had stolen the Eye of Vishnu, or whether the object resting in her satchel was actually the thing that had caught her eye in the chateau. He said nothing, knowing that he would find out the answer soon enough. Carmen Sandiego always had her reasons for doing things the way she did.

The door to Carmen's compartment opened, and before she could tell the intruder that he was in the wrong car, she found herself face-to-face with someone she had not seen in a very long time.

"Hello, Gray," Carmen said as the young man approached.

He was gangly yet handsome, with messy brown hair and broad shoulders. He spoke with a thick Australian accent. "Well, well . . ." Gray said as he closed the compartment door behind him. "Isn't this a blast from the past?"

"Blast from the past? Is someone th —"

Before Player could finish his question, Gray took out a metal rod that looked unmistakably high-tech and pressed a button on the side of it. A jolt of electricity coursed through the compartment. Carmen raised an eyebrow at Gray.

"That was a directional EMP," Gray said. "I just wiped out all your electronics. Your phone and any other communication devices are offline now, so you can forget about calling a friend for help." Carmen hoped that Player wouldn't worry.

"I know what an *electromagnetic pulse* does, Gray. I took Bellum's class too, remember?"

Carmen sat back down on the train seat. She casually

gestured toward the black satchel next to her as she said, "You didn't think I would steal it without checking for a tracking device first, did you?" Gray stared at her, unable to hide his surprise. Carmen suppressed a smile at this. "That's right. I *wanted* you to find me. I thought it was time we tied up some loose ends."

Gray angrily sat down opposite her. "*You* were the only loose end . . . until five seconds ago, when I captured the great Carmen Sandiego." He leaned forward. "Or should I call you . . . Black Sheep?"

Black Sheep. That was a name she hadn't heard in a while.

"Do you remember when we met?" Carmen asked.

"It would be a hard thing to forget," Gray responded. "It was the day we became students at VILE Academy. We're not on the island anymore. We don't have to abide by VILE's rules, so we don't have to keep our pasts a secret anymore." Gray leaned forward. "What's your story?"

"I guess there's no harm in talking about it now," Carmen said after a moment. "Why not? We have a long train ride ahead of us."

She had never told her story before. Perhaps it was time to come to terms with her past . . . what she knew of it.

CHAPTER 2

'M TOLD THAT I WAS FOUND AS A BABY ON THE SIDE OF the road somewhere just outside of Buenos Aires, Argentina. I never knew who I was or why I was left there. The only clue I had about my past was a set of Russian nesting dolls that I had been found with. You know, those painted wooden dolls of smaller and smaller size placed one inside another. Even with faded red paint and scorch marks across their sides, they were my most prized possession.

Despite not knowing who my parents were or why I was abandoned, I never felt sad about being an orphan when I was young. It might sound strange, but back then, it never occurred to me to be sad or jealous about not having the same kind of upbringing that other kids had. I made my own fun, and there was always stuff to do . . . because I was growing up in a real-life *paradise*.

I didn't grow up in an orphanage with other kids or anything like that. Instead, I grew up on the grounds of a very unusual school that was on a secluded tropical island in the middle of the ocean. Whoever found me as a baby brought me to this place called Vile Island, named after the organization it housed. The island was beautiful. Everywhere you looked, there were white sandy beaches and palm trees. The ocean was a bright sparkling blue that glistened in the sunlight. I couldn't have asked for a better place to call home. It was as though I were a princess with her own private island . . . even though I had no clue where in the world that island was.

The person who found me as a baby in Argentina must have worked for VILE. Rather than hand me over to a local orphanage, they brought me back with them to Vile Island, where I was raised by the faculty. They say it takes a village to raise a child, but in my experience, a group of five teachers on a mysterious island will do the job too.

The large gray fortress that served as VILE Academy was sleek and modern in its design. It was full of sharp angles and harsh edges that came together in ways other people might have seen as threatening. If I'd had a better understanding of the world, I might have thought there was something ominous about it.

I lived on the academy grounds, in a small room at the front of the dormitory that was somewhat separated from the students. Of course, that didn't stop me from sneaking through the main buildings and classrooms. I used to roam the halls, running around and making mischief whenever I could.

As a child, I was too young to attend the academy with the other students. I would stomp my feet and beg to go to class with the other students, but the answer was always the same. The teachers would tell me the kinds of lessons that were taught there were things that I couldn't learn until I had grown up a bit more.

Until then, I was homeschooled by nannies. I never had the same nanny for very long . . . you could say there was a revolving door of them. They came and went, never giving a reason for their sudden departures. Whenever I asked the faculty members why a nanny was leaving, I was told it was because they had work to do for VILE somewhere else. There would always be a replacement ready to step in. But I didn't mind, because these nannies were from all sorts of different places in the world, and each new nanny would teach me about the country she was from.

I learned of just about every country in the world during those early years, from the fjords of Norway to the cherry-blossom festivals of Japan. I got a taste of many different languages, like Mandarin and Swahili. These caretakers instilled in me a love of other cultures, and I knew then that I wanted to travel the world and see them all. The world outside the island seemed like such an amazing place that was just waiting for me to explore it!

One of these nannies gave me a gift. It was a map of the world. She helped me hang it above my bed. I used to lie awake at night and trace the continents with my finger, dreaming of the day when I would be able to see each and every one of them. When I told my nanny about this, she laughed and asked, "Even Antarctica?" "Yes!" I answered with glee.

Of course, I couldn't go jetting off to other countries as a little kid, so I made do with exploring the island and causing mischief in the fortress-like school that was on it.

It didn't take long for me to figure out that I was the only child on the whole island. And as I explored my surroundings, sneaking through the halls and eavesdropping on conversations, I learned that the large gray academy that stood tall among the palm trees and the crystal-clear waters wasn't just any ordinary school—it was VILE's school *for thieves.*

VILE WAS THE NAME OF A CRIMINAL SHADOW ORGANIZA-tion that operated in secret all over the world. Their network of thieves worked in every country, pulling off all kinds of thefts. There was no caper that was beyond them—from art heists to stealing space shuttles, nothing was too far-fetched for VILE. The graduates from the academy went on to become VILE's operatives and would work together to steal millions of dollars for VILE. And sometimes VILE seemed to steal just for fun.

The world's most impressive, infamous, and hard-to-catch criminals came out of VILE Academy. When it came to their operations, secrecy was always the number-one most important thing. No one in the outside world, not even the authorities, knew that VILE existed. And here I was, growing up right inside it.

It was a school unlike any other . . . and it was also all I had known. I wanted to be a part of it.

To pass the time until I was old enough to enroll in VILE Academy, I decided to create my own kind of fun. Mischief could have been my middle name.

One day, a boat was arriving on the island. This boat arrived like clockwork each year on December first. Apart from when new students came to the island, it was the only time during the year that anyone ever came from the outside world.

Cookie Booker was a stylish middle-aged woman who, aside from the boat's captain, was the only passenger on board. She was VILE's bookkeeper and came to the island once a year to deliver an electronic hard drive and upload its contents to the computer servers in the academy. Rumor had it that Cookie absolutely hated water.

On this December first, I decided to make Cookie Booker's visit a little more memorable. I crawled up onto the rocks that overlooked the boat dock, water balloons tucked carefully in my arms. I could see Cookie Booker below. She was wearing a brightly colored dress with a wide-brimmed sun hat placed at a stylish angle across her head. The captain was busy tying the boat to the docks. This was my moment.

I brought my arm back and hurled the first balloon. It curled through the air perfectly, bursting just to the left of Cookie Booker's feet. She was splashed with water, as was her turquoise handbag. I threw a second balloon, and this one didn't miss its target. Cookie Booker gave a hysterical shriek of anger.

I choked back a laugh as I realized the captain had spotted me. *Time to skedaddle,* I thought, and took off running.

I burst into the academy complex, rounding a corner as fast as my feet would take me.

Even though my heart was pounding, I was having the time of my life. I lived for thrills like these. I led the captain on a wild chase through the academy grounds. I could hear him losing his breath—I just had to keep going a little longer until I lost him for good. Then I turned the corner and felt my feet slip and slide across a wet, freshly mopped floor. I slid straight into a dead end.

I gave a nervous laugh as the captain approached me. "What strange weather!" I said. "Who knew it was going to rain today?"

"The only thing raining out there was water balloons, and you know it!"

"Is there a problem here?" asked Coach Brunt, who had appeared at the end of the hall and was eyeing the captain with a red fury. I never wanted to be on the receiving end of that look. Coach Brunt was one of the five faculty members who ran VILE Academy. She was a large Texan woman who showed brute strength in everything she did. Once, when she was angry, I saw her punch a hole straight through a brick wall.

But for some reason, Coach Brunt took a liking to me and watched over me like I imagined a mother would. I often suspected that Coach Brunt was the one who found me as a baby in Argentina, but whenever I asked her about it, she quickly changed the subject. She was always there to get me out of trouble, often referring to herself as my "Mama Bear." And this time was no exception.

As Coach Brunt glared at the captain, I blinked, just for a moment, and when I opened my eyes again, the captain was falling backwards with a dazed look in his eyes. Brunt lowered her fist to her side.

As he fell, a small metal object flew out of his pocket and skidded across the floor toward my feet. Instinctively, I reached down and picked it up before anyone saw. My heart started pounding as I realized what I had just gotten my hands on — *a cellphone!*

I HAD DISCOVERED THAT STEALING THINGS WAS REALLY fun, and getting away with it was even more exciting. Slowly, I began to pick up all kinds of thieving skills. I dreamed of the day I'd be able to become a VILE student and put those skills to the test. I would be the best thief that VILE had ever seen! And *I* would finally get to see more of the world than my tiny island.

One rainy afternoon, I was in my room, staring at the world map that was pinned to the wall. When she had given it to me, my nanny said that I could put pins in the places I traveled to mark all the spots where I had been. But it was still as empty as ever. I couldn't even put a pin in the island, since I had no idea where it was!

Suddenly one of the Russian nesting dolls on my windowsill began to shake and tremble. *An earthquake?* I wondered, and bolted upright. No. Nothing else was moving. That's when I remembered — I had hidden the captain's cellphone inside that doll!

I cautiously took the phone out from its hiding place. On the phone's screen was an image of a *white hat* that glowed as the phone vibrated. And then a text message came up on the screen: "'Better beef up your security. I got in,'" I read aloud. What on earth did that mean?

Got in where? Here? I messaged back.

The phone began to ring. I was so startled by the noise that I jumped. I stared at the phone for a moment, unsure of what to do.

I took a deep breath and answered it.

"Hello?"

"Hello," came the voice on the other side. He sounded young — much younger than me. But who was he?

"Who is this?" he asked, beating me to the question.

"Black Sheep," I answered matter-of-factly. Coach Brunt had told me that becoming a VILE operative meant giving up your personal identity. After all, it wouldn't do for authorities to be able to trace your name back to VILE if you were caught. This meant that each of the students would eventually earn his or her criminal code name.

It was a rite of passage for new recruits, and if you successfully became an operative, your code name was what you would be known as from that point forward. Since I was an orphan with no other name to go by, I was given my code name early.

Black Sheep.

"What's your *real* name?" he asked.

I was confused. *My real name?* Black Sheep was the only name I had ever known. "My name is Black Sheep," I repeated. To my surprise, the voice chuckled.

"Okay, usernames work. You can call me Player. I'm a white-hat hacker." He sounded proud of this fact, even though I didn't know what it meant.

"What's a white-hat hacker?" I asked.

"It means I have crazy-awesome hacking skills, but I use them for good," he explained. "I just hacked through twenty-seven layers of encryption to get through to you. Who should I talk to about the weak link in your security?"

"Are you pranking me right now? Where are you calling from?" I couldn't believe a little kid could hack into VILE's security.

"My bedroom. In Niagara Falls."

I gasped. In my entire life, I had never spoken to anyone outside of the island. My mind raced with excitement. "Which side of the falls are you on? The American side or the Canadian?"

"Canadian."

"You're in Ontario? That's amazing! What's it like there?"

"You really know your geography," Player responded, surprised by my interest. "It's all right here, I guess. We have computers and the internet and . . . hang on a second! Where in the world are *you?*"

I was unsure of how to answer that question, since I didn't actually know. "School," I responded with a shrug.

"What kind of school needs twenty-seven layers of encryption?" Player asked with disbelief.

I thought about how to answer him. What could I say?

"Mom's telling me to take out the trash—gotta go!" Player said, giving me an easy out. Then he added, "Black Sheep? Do you want to talk again sometime? I have *got* to get to the bottom of this twenty-seven-layer mystery."

And so began the first real friendship of my life. I wanted to know everything there was about life on the mainland. Or rather, *a* mainland, since I didn't know where my island was. Could this mean I was near Canada? No, it was too tropical on my island to be that far north.

Every day after that first call, I would sneak away to a hidden spot and talk to Player. If anyone found out about my conversations with him, my phone would be taken away, and even Coach Brunt might not be able to protect me this time. Secrecy was the number-one most important thing to VILE, after all. But I didn't care about the risks. I had made contact with the outside world!

As we talked, I learned that Player was just as curious about me as I was about him. Even though he asked plenty of questions, I never knew how to answer them.

How could I even begin to explain my life on the island? Would he even believe me if I tried? I decided it would be best to keep the details of my life, and the truth about Vile Island, a secret.

Instead I made him tell me all about Canada.

"Do you watch hockey? Does it snow there all the time? Have you seen the northern lights?" The questions came out in a single breath as we talked one afternoon.

"Slow down, Black Sheep! Umm . . . no, yes, and yes."

"I've never even seen snow," I said with a sigh. The most I could hope for on the island was some rain here or a thunderstorm there.

"Lucky! It gets old after a while. And it is *freezing!*"

Player indulged my questions and seemed to sense that I had my reasons for not telling him about my own life. He told me about Niagara Falls, about the people there, about a Canadian food called *poutine* (french fries, gravy, and cheese!) that he told me I *had* to try someday. He spent the most time telling me about the latest computer games he was playing and his latest hacking victories.

"Tell me more about white-hat hackers," I said one day.

"I started hacking because I was bored," he explained. "Then I found out about *white-hat* hacking. It's where you hack into things, but instead of doing anything bad once you've gotten in, you do good things—like how I was going to tell someone about the weaknesses in your school's security."

"I'll, uh . . . be sure to let them know."

"We have a code, you know. I've sworn to always use my powers for good."

"But where's the fun in that?" I asked, feeling confused.

"I don't know." He paused, deep in thought. "I guess it's about the challenge and proving something to yourself. If I go after the right hack, it's still really challenging . . . the *good* kind of challenging!"

ONE DAY, I WATCHED AS THE LATEST GROUP OF STUDENTS made their way into the auditorium for graduation. They had all passed their classes and earned their code names. They would be split into groups and sent off to complete their very first capers for VILE. I thought longingly of the far-off places they would go and the exciting artifacts they would steal. Maybe they would get to run through old forgotten tombs filled with booby traps, just like in the storybooks I used to read as a child.

I felt a surge of jealousy as I watched them leave, desperately wishing I could be in their shoes.

When I talked to Player that day, he could tell something was wrong.

"Wait, so you *live* at this school, but you're not a student there?" he asked after I told him how badly I wanted to be a part of the graduating class.

"Not yet. I'm too young. Everyone who comes here for the program has to be at least eighteen."

"That seems like a dumb rule."

I smiled at his attempts to cheer me up. "Yeah, it is pretty dumb," I agreed.

"I mean, you might be young, but any university would be lucky to have someone as smart as you!"

VILE Academy was nothing like a college or university, but I didn't correct him. After all, it wasn't as though I could tell him the truth. Still, what Player said gave me the spark of an idea.

"Maybe . . . maybe they can make an exception."

"What are you thinking?" he asked.

"I think it's time to prove myself. I'm going to talk to the faculty."

After my phone call with Player, I decided to do something I had never dared to do before. I found Coach Brunt and told her that I wanted to address the faculty.

I called for a *family meeting.*

In addition to Coach Brunt, each of the other faculty members who ran VILE had their own area of expertise.

First there was Dr. Saira Bellum. Dr. Bellum was a scientist from India who had a penchant for inventing elaborate devices. She was something of an oddball and always seemed to be working on a hundred things at once, which usually turned out to be a mistake, as nothing could hold her attention for very long. But despite her quirks, she was a genius. She had the ability to create anything, from mind-control devices to robots.

Then there was Countess Cleo, who was from Egypt. She had an eye for the more sophisticated side of crime, like art forgeries and jewelry thefts. If you needed lessons in how to blend in with high society, she was the one for the job. She wasn't a fan of my wild nature or mischievous pranks, and I always got the impression that she desperately wanted to tame me.

Next was Gunnar Maelstrom. He was from Scandinavia and was an intense man who could always be traced back to the stranger and more unpredictable criminal plots. He would often pull off the craziest of capers not for the profit, but because he liked the challenge. He was always playing mind tricks on his students, and even when he was being funny, it felt like there was something dark about him lurking just below the surface.

And then there was Shadowsan . . . who had zero patience for my pranks. Shadowsan was a straight-faced Japanese ninja who was a master of stealth. Rumor had it that he could creep up on you in an open field in the middle of the day and still manage to surprise you. He made it clear that he thought I didn't belong here—that the island was no place for a child. Naturally, I avoided him as much as I possibly could.

My heart racing, I walked down the long hallway toward the faculty lounge. The faculty lounge at VILE was one of the most frightening places at the academy. It was where the faculty members gathered to plan their criminal operations.

I pushed open the door and entered the large room. The sound of my footsteps echoed loudly as I made my way to stand in front of a long table. Each of the five faculty members was seated behind it, staring down at me. My heart felt like it was about to fly out of my chest, but I forced myself to look each of them in the eye.

Countess Cleo, as always, seemed bored. Beside her, Professor Maelstrom was looking me up and down, his expression as hard to read as ever. "Black Sheep, why have you requested our audience?" he asked.

I was terrified but tried my hardest not to show it. If I was going to get them on my side, I would have to appear as confident as possible. "I'm ready to enroll," I said, trying to sound sure of myself. "I know I'm not technically old enough, Professor Maelstrom, but I think I have what it takes to be a great thief . . . the best ever!" I gulped as I remembered my place and added, "In my opinion, sir."

Dr. Bellum thought carefully about my request, her wild eyes darting from me to the other faculty members. "Black Sheep may be young, but she has had more training at her age than any other recruit. Even if only by being around the academy for so long."

Brunt clapped a huge hand on Bellum's shoulder in agreement. "Dr. Bellum's right. Little Black Sheep is ready to run with the big dogs."

Countess Cleo leaned back in her seat, unconvinced. "I am not looking forward to dealing with Black Sheep's lack of manners in a classroom setting," she said. I winced. I should have known that the elegant Countess Cleo might bring up my mischievous behavior.

"Precisely why she may be overdue for properly supervised training," Maelstrom countered. "And what do you think, Shadowsan?"

My hands began shaking again as I waited for Shadowsan to speak. He looked at me intensely, and I knew that he would be the hardest person to persuade.

After an agonizing moment of silence, Shadowsan said, "We train the best thieves in the world in these halls. It is not a place for someone as undisciplined and unruly as Black Sheep. She is not ready to be one of the forty thieves."

I stared down at my shoes as Shadowsan's words hung heavy in the air. Each year, these five faculty members would handpick a select group of forty up-and-coming criminals from the world at large. These recruits had already shown some serious talent for thievery, and they usually even had their own areas of expertise. Some would be masters of disguise; others were amateur cat burglars. And what was I? A prankster? I worried that Shadowsan was right, but I also knew I could be a great thief if they would just give me the chance!

"We've never had such a strong case for advanced placement until now," Coach Brunt said. I looked back up, and her eyes met mine. She winked at me, and I smiled at her despite my nervousness. "Black Sheep has already learned a great deal, and I have a feelin' in my gut that she'll be one of our star pupils if we give her a chance. Besides . . . majority vote rules, Shadowsan."

"All in favor?" asked Maelstrom.

I held my breath as Brunt and Bellum raised their hands, followed by Maelstrom and then Cleo.

Four votes! I had done it!

Shadowsan leaned forward, towering over me from his position behind the table. "You'd better be certain that becoming a professional thief is what you truly want, Black Sheep, for once you go down this road, there is no turning back." I did my best to hold Shadowsan's gaze. I was determined not to let him know how much he intimidated me, but inside I was terrified.

Was this what I wanted? *Of course it is,* I told myself. *You're going to be the best thief the world has ever seen!*

"Instructor Shadowsan, I want this more than anything," I told him. This time, I didn't have to pretend to be confident.

From that moment forward, I was taking on a life of crime. And class was about to begin.

CHAPTER 3

I HAD SPENT MY ENTIRE CHILDHOOD WATCHING AS each year a group of recruits from all over the globe came and went from the island. Now it was finally my turn.

"I got in!" I told Player. I could barely believe it.

"Nice going, Black Sheep!"

"Talking to you made me realize that I should take matters into my own hands."

"I'll bet you won't have much time for these chats once you start classes," he said.

"Don't be ridiculous. You're my best friend, Player. My *only* friend," I said, and meant it.

THE FIRST DAY OF ORIENTATION WAS ONE OF THE MOST exciting of my life. I was the youngest of all the recruits by far, and one of the smallest, too. But I didn't let it get to me. Soon enough, I thought, I would show them that I was every bit as good as they were. *Better,* even.

We sat in the auditorium, all forty of us, in the olive-green-and-khaki student uniforms that I had seen so many other students wear before me. I wore mine proudly, beaming with confidence, while Coach Brunt gave the introductions that I had waited so long to hear.

Brunt stood behind a podium while a large screen glowed with the VILE logo behind her. "Welcome to VILE training academy," she began. "You have each been selected for our one-year program due to the extraordinary potential you have demonstrated." Brunt gestured to the VILE logo, its sharp edges just right for a criminal organization. "VILE . . . It stands for Valuable Imports, Lavish Exports. We traffic stolen goods to the four corners of the globe."

As Brunt spoke, I tried to steal glances at my fellow classmates. I had a hard time making out their faces in the dark. Who were these people I would be spending the next year of my life with?

"While you are here, you are to have no contact with the outside world." Brunt picked up a cellphone from the podium and crushed it in her hand. When she opened her hand again, the phone was nothing more than a mangled mess of plastic and metal.

A few students sounded disappointed. I remained as

emotionless as possible. Coach Brunt had no idea that I had my secret cellphone . . . my link to Player and the outside world. If any of the faculty found out, I might be expelled from the academy before I even started.

"You are also to keep your life stories to yourselves," Brunt continued. "This is a new beginning for you. That means you are to use first names only, until you have earned your code names." Coach Brunt smiled at me from the stage. "Isn't that right, little Lambkins?" I blushed a deep red. "Lambkins" was Coach Brunt's affectionate nickname for me and had been since I was an infant . . . but it wasn't something I wanted to be called in front of all my new classmates! I tried to smile back at her as I sank a little lower in my seat.

From behind me, there was a loud snort. "Lambkins? I didn't know this place had a mascot." I whirled around to face the owner of the Australian accent behind me. With anger rising, I grabbed him roughly by the shirt collar and pulled him close. "Only Coach Brunt calls me Lambkins! To you, I'm Black Sheep! Do you understand? Nod if you understand!"

"Whoa . . . I mean . . . yes! Just let me go." I did as he asked, slamming him back into his seat for good measure. Out of the corner of my eye, I could have sworn I saw Coach Brunt smiling at me from the stage.

After orientation, it was time for me to meet my new

group of roommates. Instead of my own private room, I was going to be rooming with my fellow recruits in the dormitory. I wasn't sure if I was excited or annoyed at the prospect. I had lived as an only child—the only child on the *whole island*—for so long that I was unsure of whether or not I would be able to make friends.

At the dormitory, we received our room assignments, and I was told I would be sharing a room with four other students. I hurried and found I was the first one there. Two boys arrived, followed by a girl. They each waved an awkward hello as they entered, which I nervously returned. I waited for my last roommate to arrive, secretly hoping it would be a third girl so we would outnumber the boys. The door opened, and in walked the Australian boy I had yelled at in the auditorium.

We stared at each other for a moment, and then I gave a small "Harrumph!" and turned to finish putting away my things. The Australian chuckled with a shake of his head and went to do the same.

It took only minutes for the rule forbidding us from telling one another about our past to go out the window.

"I was working as a junior electrician at the Sydney

Opera House in Australia," said the one who called himself Graham.

"Australia? You mean *down under?*" I asked, my eyes widening. His earlier offense was quickly becoming a distant memory.

"Yeah, what of it?" He seemed taken aback by my excitement.

"Have you held a koala? Do you play rugby? Have you seen any great white sharks?"

"I'll uhh . . . get back to you on that. Anyway, one day," Graham continued, "a light bulb went on. I could make a far better living stealing from wealthy opera-goers than I could as a measly electrician. I still play around with electricity, of course — only now I do it so I can steal things." We had gotten off on the wrong foot, but Graham spoke with a laid-back tone that made him easy to like.

"I am Jean-Paul," said a tall guy with an athletic build. He had a thick French accent. I quickly stopped myself from asking him a dozen questions about Europe. "I like *heights.* I'm the greatest rock climber in the world, you know. The higher, the better, I say. One day I got bored with climbing around for no reason, and I decided to apply my passion for rock climbing to high-rise heists."

The shorter, more muscular guy sitting next to Jean-Paul nodded in understanding. "I am Antonio," he said with a gentle Spanish accent. He seemed friendly and mellow, whereas Jean-Paul came off as gruff and serious. "My expertise is navigating small spaces. Jean-Paul here might like the high ground, but I like the *low*. There is no bank vault that I can't burrow into from below." Antonio suddenly looked wistful as he stared off into the distance. "Digging . . . tunneling . . . feeling the earth between my toes . . ."

"Yuck!" said an American girl to my left. She flipped her blond hair back and looked around at the four of us like we were lucky to be in her presence. "I'm Sheena. Hi. I like shoplifting." Graham rolled his eyes at this, and Sheena glared back at him defensively. "I have a thing for bling."

Sheena looked toward the Russian nesting dolls I had just placed by my bed and turned back to me. "Is this where you keep your jewelry, little girl?"

Instinctively I stepped in front of them, guarding my territory. I might have been younger and smaller than the rest of my roommates, but I was not about to let myself be bullied by a roommate who had a thing for shoplifting.

"Please don't touch my stuff," I said firmly.

Sheena raised an eyebrow. She could tell she was getting to me, and she reached toward the dolls. "What, those?"

I clenched a fist at my side. "I said, keep your paws off!" I could feel my anger rising, and I knew that it was about to come out. Graham quickly stepped in front of Sheena, giving a lighthearted chuckle. "Play nice, princess. We all have to room together."

Sheena looked for a moment as though she was going to make another move for the dolls, then thought better of it. "It's probably just cheap jewelry, anyway," she said with a huff as she stepped away. Graham smiled at me, and I couldn't help but smile back.

THE NEXT DAY, CLASSES STARTED. I WOKE UP FEELING more excited than I had ever been in my life. This was the day my career as a thief was finally going to begin.

Graham noticed my excitement as we made our way toward our first class. "You're really raring to go, aren't you, Black Sheep?" he said. He was sporting an easygoing smile that I would come to be very familiar with. I shrugged. The last thing I wanted was to seem desperate or overeager. I tried to put on an air of confidence instead.

"Are you really going to go by *Graham* while you're here?" I asked.

"What, you don't like it?"

"It's not very . . . cool," I explained knowingly. "What about Gray? That's way cooler than Graham!"

"Gray, huh? That's not bad." He cast a sly look down at me. "But nothing's better than Lambkins."

"You're right, but don't be jealous. And remember— it's Black Sheep to you."

I felt someone bump hard into my shoulder and looked up to see Sheena scowling at us as she pushed on ahead. "Black and Gray. That's *too* cute," she said with a smirk. I simply ignored her and made my way into our first class.

I had seen each of the classrooms many times while roaming the academy halls. But I had never known what lessons were taught within.

Finally it's my turn, I thought as I took my seat on a mat inside Shadowsan's classroom for first period: Stealth 101.

The room was decorated in a minimalist Japanese style. I gazed around at the traditional decorations— there were bonsai trees and Japanese fans and delicate folding screens that lined the walls. My eyes moved to a long samurai sword that rested on a stone pedestal behind the teacher's desk. *Are we going to be using that?* I wondered, feeling giddy with excitement.

Shadowsan took his place at the head of the classroom. Just for an instant, I could have sworn he flashed an angry look in my direction, but I blinked, and the moment had passed. I shrugged it off. I wasn't about to let anything get in the way of acing all my classes and being the best student this school had ever seen.

Shadowsan reached into his pocket and pulled out an origami sheep, carefully and crisply folded. "Origami, the art of paper folding, is the best way to practice and perfect a nimble touch," he said as he set the sheep down on a table next to a set of other paper figures. "Essential for the successful picking of pockets."

Moments later, we were all given our own sets of origami paper. I focused hard on mine. I folded each edge carefully, as though it were an intricate puzzle to be solved.

I looked around at my classmates. Their origami, if you could call it that, all looked like crumpled pieces of homework that the family dog had gotten its paws on.

Not mine, though. Mine was a flawlessly folded unicorn. The meticulous folding and precise movements of the fingers came as naturally to me as breathing.

Shadowsan passed by, and I held up my origami toward him proudly. He kept walking, his expression completely blank. *I'll bet he was impressed,* I thought. *He just didn't want to show it.*

"Nice rhinoceros," said Gray. His origami looked like a piece of paper that had been spat out of a lawn mower. Jean-Paul and Antonio weren't doing much better. Jean-Paul's goat looked more like a toad, and Antonio had crumpled up his mole in frustration, leaving it a wrinkled mess.

"It's a unicorn," I corrected. "What's yours, anyway?"

"It's supposed to be a kangaroo," Gray said dryly. "This class is Stealth 101. I heard our instructor used to be a ninja. When is he going to show us some moves?"

"I'll find out," I said as my hand shot up in the air. Gray and I were beginning to become friends. It was an experience that was completely new to me, and I found myself wanting to impress him and the others.

I caught the attention of Shadowsan. He turned to me slowly, raising his eyebrow ever so slightly at my raised hand. "Instructor Shadowsan, sir," I blurted out, "aren't we going to learn how to use *that?*" I pointed at the sword resting on the pedestal.

He gestured to the sword behind him. "The sword? That is an antique. It is only for looking at." He turned his gaze back to me, and I flinched under his critical look. "But if you wish to play with toys, Coach Brunt will be teaching you the art of self-defense."

There were snickers from the other students. Sheena was laughing the loudest. I looked across the room to see her grinning triumphantly. She looked all too happy about Shadowsan putting me in my place.

I walked quickly to my next class, determined to do better in this one. The class was Coach Brunt's Combat and Weaponry. It was held in Brunt's gymnasium, where we had access to everything from punching bags to long wooden sticks, called *bo staffs,* that were used for practice fighting. It was a room that hung heavy with an air of athleticism and discipline.

I had always been fast and nimble on my feet, but I would be going up against students who were twice my size. I was suddenly noticing how short I was compared to everyone else. I tried to calm my nerves as we made our way inside. It didn't matter if the other students were bigger or older than me, I decided. I was going to use my own strengths against them.

Coach Brunt sized us up, one by one. She gave me a reassuring nod when she saw me in line. "In this class, I'm going to drill you hard — understand?" she yelled out as she walked back and forth in front of us. "Don't ever let your guard down! When you're in the field, no one's going to go easy on you, so I don't want to see you going easy on each other!"

She picked up a set of bo staffs and tossed them to us. "The first rule of self-defense . . ." Brunt yelled in her thick Southern accent. ". . . Always protect the face!"

We split up into pairs as Brunt told us, "Do your worst!"

I held my bo staff tightly in my hands and lunged toward Gray. He sidestepped me easily. "Too slow," he teased. Before he had a chance to come at me, I snarled and lunged toward him a second time. He was taken aback, just as I'd hoped. He once again managed to avoid me, clumsily this time. While he stumbled, I did a low spin-kick that took out his feet, and he fell to the floor. "Whoa!" he exclaimed. "Not bad, Black Sheep!"

Gray and I traded blows with our staffs for a while. Next to us, Antonio and Jean-Paul were doing the same, with Antonio eventually taking Jean-Paul down by barreling into him with his shoulder.

Gray nudged me and gestured across the room. "Who's the bloke that Sheena's fighting with?"

Sheena was paired with a quiet student I had seen at orientation but not spoken to. He was distractedly looking around the gymnasium, his back turned slightly toward Sheena. Before I had a chance to warn him, Sheena jabbed her bo staff into him, knocking him flat on his back.

I quickly walked over, extended my hand to him, and helped him up. "You okay?" I asked. He said nothing, giving only a slight shrug and a nod.

"I didn't realize this was a *team-building* exercise," Sheena said as she took a swing at me with her staff. In a flash, I caught her staff with my hand and pulled on it. She went tumbling down with a squeal.

"That's how it's done, Lambkins!" Brunt said with a grin, and she winked at me proudly. Sheena hissed angrily as she got to her feet, glaring daggers at me.

Soon enough it was time to move on to Countess

Cleo's class. I was unsure of what to expect from a class called Criminal Etiquette, but I knew that Cleo would be all too eager to make a more polite person out of me if given the chance. In her eyes, I was a wild little child —and she wasn't completely wrong.

Cleo's classroom was a place of elegance, with beautiful patterned curtains hanging from the windows and priceless artwork arranged in perfectly positioned spots on the walls.

"In this class, you will learn to distinguish the finer things from the . . . *not*-so-finer things." Cleo strutted to the front of the classroom like a model on a runway. "A forgery is a fake. Something that is copied to look like the real thing. It will not do for you to steal a pile of fake diamonds instead of the real deal." She made a face of utter disgust. "If you want to be successful criminals instead of petty thieves, you will have to learn how to pass within high society and how to tell the difference between what's valuable and what's not.

"Pop quiz!" Cleo said as she gestured to two identical vases on the table next to her. The vases each had very detailed blue-and-white flower designs wrapping around their sides. "One of these vases is discount flea-market garbage," she explained. "The other is a genuine Ming vase from the Jiajing period, valued at three hundred thousand dollars. Which would you steal? Anyone?"

"Oh! I know!" Sheena called out, waving her hand in the air. Countess Cleo gave a nod in her direction. Sheena stood up with a smirk. She leaped down the aisle and did a series of handsprings that sent her bounding toward the front of the classroom. The final handspring sent her up in the air and over the vases.

She grabbed one of them as she landed, a triumphant look on her face. "This one!" Sheena cried proudly, enjoying all the attention she was receiving.

The second vase wobbled on the table, then—

SMASH!

It fell to the floor, bursting into a hundred pieces. Countess Cleo winced. "Tragically," she said, "you would be wrong."

Sheena raised the vase she was holding, and the price tag on the bottom, reading ninety-nine cents, was visible to all of us. "She was so sure of herself!" I snickered to Gray, and we burst out laughing. Sheena shot us a look so fiery, it would have fried an egg.

After Criminal Etiquette, we moved on to Diabolical Masterminding with Maelstrom. Of all the faculty members, he had always been the most unpredictable while I was growing up on the island. He certainly seemed strange, but I was intrigued by his unusual attitude and curious about what he might teach us.

On either side of his classroom were two massive fish

tanks with bright sea creatures that swam slowly through the water. Beyond one of the tanks, a skeleton was on display, and it felt as though it were looking right at me. Maelstrom paced in front of it, his hands clasped behind his back.

"To properly perform a bait and switch," Maelstrom said as he held a velvet sack high in his hands, "the objects should be of equal weight and size." He reached a hand into the sack and pulled out a large stack of money. "A volunteer, please?"

This time it was Antonio's turn to walk to the front of the class.

Maelstrom returned the money to the sack and handed it to Antonio. "Whatever you do," Maelstrom instructed, "hold the bag tightly! As tightly as you can."

"I am regretting this decision," I heard Antonio say under his breath.

Maelstrom casually walked past him. We all watched, our eyes glued to the sack that Antonio held in his hands. Maelstrom then stepped away from Antonio, holding a second, identical sack. "And there you have . . . *the switch!*"

Maelstrom reached into his own sack to reveal the stack of money. Antonio reached into the sack he was holding. "What is this?" he cried. He looked totally grossed out as he lifted up a fistful of squirming worms.

"That, my dear boy, would be the bait!"

Maelstrom gave a chilling chuckle. Some of the students nervously joined in. Antonio quickly stuffed the worms back into the bag and took his seat, wiping his hands on his pants. "That was disgusting," he told Jean-Paul.

"This guy is insane!" I heard Sheena hiss behind me.

"Insane? Or a genius?" Jean-Paul asked quietly. "He switched those bags while all of us were watching, and none of us noticed a thing!"

The last class of the day was Gadgetry and Tech with Dr. Bellum. There were the usual laboratory stations with beakers and basic science instruments, but then I began to gaze around at the wide range of strange devices and inventions. I had never seen anything like them before. Some were twisted into crazy shapes, and others were covered in endless rows of buttons and control panels. Given Dr. Bellum's eccentric nature, I knew there was no telling what they were used for.

"Never underestimate the power of science when you are out in the field," Bellum began, her wild eyes moving from one student to another. "Science can take out an alarm system. Or fill a room with toxic nerve gas that will stop your enemies in their tracks."

Bellum walked to the wall and took down a long metal

rod. It was not unlike the bo staff that we had been fighting with earlier in the day, only it seemed to be made of polished steel and electronics.

"Take, for example, my latest invention . . . the *crackle rod!*" Bellum turned a dial on the rod's side, and the invention hummed to life, buzzing with the electricity. I saw Gray lean forward. He looked like he was under a spell.

Bellum turned the rod to show us the dial on the side of it. "Settings can be adjusted here. Directional EMP, stun mode, and so on. An EMP, for those of you who don't know, is an *electromagnetic pulse*. It can take out any electronics as far as its range extends. Now, if you turn the dial *all* the way up . . ." Dr. Bellum cranked the dial as far as it would go. She aimed the rod directly at a crash-test dummy hanging at the far end of the classroom. With the press of a button—

ZAP!

A beam of electrical energy tore through the air and hit the dummy right in the chest. Murmurs rippled throughout the classroom as smoke poured from where the dummy had been just a moment before. It was now nothing more than charred remains on the floor.

Bellum laughed, thrilled with the results. I looked to my left and saw Gray staring at the crackle rod, his jaw slack.

"You like it?" I asked.

"Like it? More like *love* it!"

"I'll steal it for you later," I promised with a wink.

LATER THAT WEEK, I SNUCK INTO THE QUAD AND HID behind a row of hedges. Talking to Player was risky with so many students around, but it was a risk worth taking. I couldn't wait to tell him about the start of school!

There was a ringing, and then the familiar white-hat graphic appeared on the phone's screen.

"Player!"

"Yo, Black Sheep!" Player sounded just as excited to connect with me as I was with him.

"You'll never guess how my first day went! There were crackle rods, and worms, and fighting—"

"What? You're messing with me, right?"

"Don't worry, it was all part of class!"

"Well, that makes it okay, I guess," Player said sarcastically.

I looked ahead of me and saw Gray. He was looking around, as though searching for something or someone. After I poked my head out of the bushes, Gray waved to me.

"Black Sheep! There you are. I was looking for you. C'mon, mate!"

"Just dropped my pen — be right there!" I called, ducking back into the bush for a moment.

"Who's that?" Player asked.

"Graham. Well, I like to call him Gray. He's from *down under!* Where kangaroos live! He's my best friend."

"Oh." There was a sadness in Player's voice that I had never heard before, and I quickly tried to make things right.

"My best *school* friend. You know how it is, right?"

"Not really. I'm homeschooled," Player explained.

"He's actually more like a big brother. I've got to run. I'm going to be late for Criminal Etiquette."

"Wait . . . what kind of school do you go to?"

CHAPTER 4

A S THE DAYS PASSED, MY CLASSMATES AND I STUD-
ied hard and trained even harder. We learned how
to slide from ropes down the side of a building
and use a blade that could cut through glass to easily get
inside a locked window. Cleo made sure we knew which
types of paints artists from different time periods used so
we could fake priceless paintings. Shadowsan trained us
to be able to walk silently across creaky wooden floors.

As we trained, the specialties of each of my classmates soon became evident. It was becoming more and
more apparent with each passing day why they had been
selected for VILE's elite program.

One day, in Brunt's class, we were taking part in a
difficult training exercise. I tried to concentrate as I slid
down from the ceiling rafters on thin climbing ropes. All
around me, the other students were doing the same. "Your
goal is to be the first one to reach the target!" Brunt yelled

to us. The target was a briefcase that was suspended in the air twenty feet off the floor.

I was the first to make it from the rafters to the floor. I quickly grabbed a pair of long metal stilts from where they were leaning against the wall. "These stilts," Brunt explained, "will help you to get up to higher places when there's nothing else around. Use them to get to the target!" I hurriedly strapped them to my legs and tried to stand up. My legs were wobbling back and forth wildly. I took a shaky step forward, and then another.

I slowly but surely tried to make my way to the hanging briefcase, but it was impossible for me to find my balance on the thin metal stilts, and I fell backwards.

"Aahh!" I cried out, and reached for something to stop my fall. As I flew through the air, I managed to catch on to one of the climbing ropes and held on tightly. I could hear Sheena laughing at me, even though she hadn't yet made it down from the ceiling rafters. *Let's see someone else do better,* I thought.

As I lowered myself to the ground, I heard a pair of feet land on the floor next to me and turned to see Jean-Paul. He was examining the stilts. "They're for getting the briefcase," I reminded him. He tossed them aside. "I do not need these," he said matter-of-factly.

The entire class stopped what they were doing and watched in stunned silence as Jean-Paul bounded up the wall toward the briefcase. He snatched it easily from the air, then sat down on a window ledge twenty feet above us.

Coach Brunt clapped slowly, a smile spreading across her face. "Not bad. You jumped on up there like a mountain goat, didn't you?"

"Mountain goat?" Jean-Paul pondered this for a moment. "I like that."

Jean-Paul opened the briefcase and poured out handfuls of paper confetti.

"All that for some confetti?" he asked as he jumped straight down to the gymnasium floor and landed easily on his feet.

"The real prizes come *after* graduation," Brunt told him with a shrug. "And y'all better clean that confetti up."

THE FOLLOWING WEEK, GRAY AND I WERE PLAYING CHESS in the study room when suddenly Jean-Paul burst in. He looked concerned.

"What's wrong, mate?" Gray asked, seeing the look on Jean-Paul's face.

"It is Antonio! He is missing! Black Sheep, you know this island better than anyone. Do you know where he may have gone?"

Gray and I quickly agreed to help Jean-Paul look for his friend.

The three of us looked throughout the academy halls and classrooms, even daring to poke our heads into the faculty lounge. We checked the beaches, thinking he might want to burrow in the sand, but had no luck there, either.

After hours of searching, we agreed to take a break. I thought I knew every inch of the island, yet I had no idea where he could have gotten to. As we sat on the steps leading up to the school, I heard a haunting chuckle coming from the entrance.

I quickly ran toward the sound. Gray and Jean-Paul were close behind. We found Professor Maelstrom standing in the lobby. "Professor Maelstrom, sir, have you seen Antonio?"

"Oh, yes!"

Jean-Paul looked up, surprised. "You have? Where is he?"

"I'm putting his skills to the test. He gets extra credit if he can tunnel underneath the entire island," Maelstrom said with a sinister smile. "He should be popping up any second now . . . if he actually did it, that is. There's always the possibility that he could have gotten stuck or trapped somewhere."

Jean-Paul looked worried. But a moment later, we felt

the floor beneath us tremble and shake. Right where the VILE logo was engraved into the floor, the ground caved in, and a large drill with a sharp spinning top burst into the air. We all jumped back as Antonio pulled himself out of the ground, covered from head to toe in dirt and grinning wildly.

Professor Maelstrom laughed. He seemed delighted.

"Excellent! Well done. You dug as fast as a little mole. And for your prize . . . You don't have to volunteer in my class ever again!"

Antonio breathed a sigh of relief as he brushed rocks and dirt from his shoulders.

"Thank you, sir. But the real prize is having succeeded."

GRAY HAD QUICKLY BECOME DR. BELLUM'S FAVORITE STUDENT. He spent all his free afternoons in her classroom coming up with new ways for VILE operatives to use electricity on heists and helping her improve her scientific devices.

One day I walked into Bellum's class to find myself staring at an elaborate laser grid that filled the entire room. The security lasers crisscrossed every inch of the room in lines of bright red light. There was a distinct sound of buzzing electricity in the air.

"Black Sheep! Check it out!" Gray called to me proudly from the other end of the room. "Come here. I want to show you something!"

"Um, hello? I can't come over there when there are a hundred lasers in the way!"

"Oh, these? They're harmless!" Gray began to walk through the laser field. To my surprise, no alarms sounded, and the lasers themselves seemed to be nothing more than red lights. "It's something I've been working on," he explained. "If you come across a security grid when you're stealing out in the field, you can use this device. It deactivates the real security grid and replaces it with a fake one! The lasers are harmless and won't set off any alarms. But guards won't be able to tell that anything's different!"

"Not bad, Gray. You know, for an electrician," I teased, but I was impressed.

"Well, as long as the great Lambkins approves, I'll take that as a positive result."

ONE AFTERNOON, SHADOWSAN SURPRISED US WITH A new challenge in his class.

We watched as he set down two large clay jars on a bench. He then began to slowly fill each of them with grains of rice. The class looked on nervously, knowing that a difficult test would be in store for us.

"A volunteer, please," Shadowsan said, his expression as hard to read as ever. No one volunteered. "Sheena and Black Sheep. Come to the front."

I walked confidently down the aisle, even as Sheena attempted to knock me off balance by pushing me aside. "Out of my way, little lamb. This is *my* time to shine," she said.

I ignored her. Whatever Shadowsan had prepared for us, I was ready for it. I had been waiting for a chance to prove that I was the best student in the class, and I was not about to let Sheena get in the way of an opportunity like this.

"Inside each of these jars of rice are a dozen little diamonds. You are each to try to find as many diamonds as you can in two minutes. Your time starts . . . now."

Sheena and I dove our hands into the jars. Sheena haphazardly began scooping rice out of the jars and dumping it on the floor. I took a different approach. I carefully began feeling for the different shape and texture of the diamonds among the grains of rice.

Time was ticking down quickly, and soon the buzzer rang.

"Aha!" Sheena cried, opening her palm triumphantly to reveal a single diamond.

"I didn't know we were supposed to stop at one," I said as I opened my own hand to show the seven diamonds I had found.

I looked up at Shadowsan, waiting patiently for him to say something . . . to congratulate me. Instead he simply frowned.

"There were a dozen diamonds in each jar. I do not see a dozen in front of me. You will have to do better than that."

"WHAT DOES HE HAVE AGAINST YOU?" GRAY ASKED AS WE left Shadowsan's classroom.

"I got seven times as many diamonds as Sheena! No one else could have done as well as I did!" I said as I kicked a locker in frustration. "He knows it, too!" I didn't understand Shadowsan's hatred toward me, and I never had.

"Don't let him get to you," Gray said reassuringly. "Everyone knows you're the best thief here. I'll bet Shadowsan knows it too . . . even if he doesn't want to admit it."

"Aww! Is Lambkins sad she didn't get the teacher's approval?" Sheena teased as she passed us.

I spun around to face her, feeling a white-hot anger

rising up inside me. "Only my friends can call me Lambkins!" I shouted.

Sheena paused in front of me, her hand on her hip. "What are you going to do about it . . . Lambkins?"

I balled my hands into fists at my side. But before I could make a move, I felt a calming hand on my shoulder. "She's not worth it, Black Sheep," said Gray. Deep down, I knew he was right, and I walked away.

I STILL CHECKED IN WITH PLAYER AS OFTEN AS I COULD, but it was proving more and more difficult with the busy class schedule and the prying eyes of other students and faculty always around me.

I had a close call when Antonio burrowed up out of the ground close to where I was hiding in the hedges. I had to pretend that I was stopping to smell the roses, which, much to my amazement, he actually bought. He even offered pointers on how to dig deep into the ground, since, according to him, that was the only way to *really* become one with the earth.

To avoid a repeat of that little adventure, I crept into the supply closet one afternoon and took out a few fishing hooks.

I then snuck into Coach Brunt's gymnasium. I could see Brunt's silhouette in her office. I did my best to slide carefully along the wall until I made it to where the gym equipment was stored. I took a few bungee cords and slung them over my back, then quickly made my escape. *I could turn the stolen goods in for extra credit,* I thought, until I remembered why I had taken them in the first place.

Sitting outside, I tied a cord to one of the hooks, using the knots Coach Brunt had taught me to tie when I was a child. Then I flung the hook up to the roof. It took me a few tries, but soon it caught and stayed secure. I tested my weight, then began to climb up the side of the building. My makeshift grappling hook was working perfectly!

As soon as I was on the rooftop, I pulled the grappling hook up and admired my handiwork. *Not bad,* I decided.

From up here, I could see the entire island. Students were making their way across the quad. Some were practicing their criminal skills and training together; others were playing games and gossiping. In the distance, the ocean sparkled a deep turquoise blue.

It was the perfect place to talk to Player. I could see everything, but as long as I lay low, no one could see me.

I dialed his number, and as always, the white-hat logo came up onscreen.

"Player! Any luck?" I asked hurriedly. Player had been working hard to try to determine where in the world I was. We had hoped he could figure out my location by hacking into VILE's computer servers.

"Bad news, Black Sheep."

"Nothing?"

"Whatever school you're at . . . they *really* don't want to be found. I've never seen anything like it!"

"Maybe it's in the South Pacific. Or off the coast of New Zealand!"

Player was silent for a moment as he thought long and hard. "Doesn't it bother you that you're at a school and you don't even know where it is?"

"Well, of course I'm curious. But it's not like I'll be here forever. When I graduate, I'm going to travel the entire world. Besides, it's a . . . special kind of school. Is that really so crazy?"

"Like I said, I'm homeschooled. I wouldn't really know what's crazy."

CHAPTER 5

ALONG WITH TRAINING HARD, MY ROOMMATES and I would also *play* hard. I still loved pulling pranks and being a general mischief-maker — and now I had friends to help with my wild plans.

December first came around, and, like clockwork, the bookkeeper's boat was pulling into the dock. I was once again armed with water balloons, only this time, I had convinced my roommates to help me.

Jean-Paul, Antonio, and Gray were armed with more water balloons than I would ever be able to carry by myself. Even Sheena had come along, though I suspected it was because she didn't want to be left out of anything and not because she was getting into the spirit of things.

We crouched down in our hiding spot and looked at the docks below. The five of us watched and waited carefully as Cookie Booker made her way off the boat and onto the docks. I saw the captain whose cellphone I had stolen, and I wondered if he had ever reported it as missing.

The bookkeeper was dressed in a bright yellow-and-black outfit, looking every bit like a human bumblebee. Gray nudged me. "Bookkeeper? More like the *bee*keeper, am I right?" he offered with a grin.

I snickered, then caught sight of Sheena eyeing us. *Forget her,* I thought. *It's almost showtime.*

"See the handbag she's carrying?" I whispered to the others quietly, gesturing to Cookie Booker's yellow-and-black-striped purse. "It only *looks* like a purse. It's actually a hard drive! It's loaded with super-classified information gathered by VILE operatives all over the world! Apparently the information on the hard drive is everything VILE needs to plan all its heists and capers for the next year. It's where they keep all their data about ongoing operations and new targets . . . it's top-*top*-secret stuff." I was talking fast, unable to contain my excitement.

I had only heard rumors of the hard drive's existence a year before. "It's too important to risk uploading from a remote location, so they make her carry the hard drive onto the island by hand," I explained. "She travels here by boat to avoid detection, but—get this—she's afraid of water!" Even Jean-Paul and Antonio laughed at this.

"That is hilarious," Jean-Paul said with a grin.

"And smart," added Antonio. "What if someone hacked into it?"

I gulped, thinking of Player. With awesome skills like

his, I had no doubt that he could hack into the hard drive if he had access to it.

"Ready to have some fun?" I asked them with a mischievous grin. "Take aim . . . and bring the rain!"

The five of us brought our arms back. On my signal, we hurled the balloons, and they arched through the air like cannonballs.

Cookie Booker looked up toward the sky and shielded her face, but it was too late — the water balloons were already coming down around her, one by one. She yelped and shrieked as water splattered the ground around her fashionable shoes. "Black Sheep!" she yelled angrily. "I know it's you!"

Laughing loudly, the five of us took off running. I was relieved to see that even Sheena seemed to finally be having a bit of fun as she giggled while she ran. "Did you see her face? Now, *that* was hysterical!"

"I know, right? Miss Bumblebee went for a swim!"

I was leading the group away from the scene of the crime. We ran across the grounds, sprinting through the quad and toward the academy to safety. What I had failed to see was that I was leading the group right into the path of Vlad and Boris, the VILE "Cleaners." They were the school's janitors, but rumor had it they also helped the faculty with other, more secretive matters. I looked up to see their hulking frames blocking our path into the school.

I skidded to a halt, my shoes screeching loudly on the floor.

Boris was much taller than the stout Vlad, who crossed his arms against his chest as he looked at the five of us. In unison, Vlad and Boris each raised a disapproving eyebrow. This was bad, and I knew it. Vlad and Boris were the eyes and ears of the faculty members. Anything the two of them saw would certainly be reported.

"We were just . . . going for a jog!" I said quickly. "Nothing like brisk exercise and fresh air, right, fellas?"

Boris nodded in Sheena's direction, and I saw that she was still holding a handful of colorful water balloons. She quickly tried to hide them behind her back but fumbled. The water balloons went spilling onto the ground with loud *SPLATS!*

"Nice going, Sheena," Gray groaned as Antonio clapped a hand to his forehead.

VLAD AND BORIS WASTED NO TIME IN BRINGING THE FIVE of us before the faculty. The last time I had been in this room, I had asked to be enrolled in VILE Academy. Now I was here as a student facing punishment for my silly pranks. Would the faculty regret putting their faith in me?

The faculty members towered over us. Beneath our

feet was the huge VILE logo. I could see Sheena nervously shuffling her feet back and forth.

I took a deep breath and looked up at the faces of my instructors. "I take full responsibility. It was all my idea. They didn't even want to come along." It was true, after all. They never would have thrown those water balloons if it weren't for me. I was the one who had roped my friends into these childish games of mine.

"Did I not tell you Black Sheep was immature and reckless?" Shadowsan asked scornfully. "I recommend expulsion."

I felt my stomach drop. *Expulsion!* Over a few water balloons? I tried to come up with a response, but my mind was racing so fast that I couldn't think clearly. Were they really going to expel me? Just when I had finally started to prove myself?

"Esteemed faculty, with all due respect . . . Black Sheep isn't to blame. We egged her on," Gray said. I stared at him.

"No, we didn't," Sheena hissed quietly. Gray quickly elbowed her in the ribs.

"It is true," Antonio said. Jean-Paul looked surprised. "Yes, I am taking the high ground for once," Antonio whispered to his friend.

I watched as the faculty members turned to talk quietly among themselves. Though I strained to hear what they were saying, I could catch only pieces of their conversation. "We can't expel the whole herd of 'em," came a clear Texan voice.

"All in favor?" asked Maelstrom. I swallowed hard, worried about what it was they had just agreed upon.

"If you insist upon acting like children . . ." began Shadowsan. My heart pounded. ". . . You shall be treated like children. You are all sentenced to . . . detention. For one week."

Detention? Now, that I could live with.

"Ugh, this is the worst! It's like we're in grade school!" Sheena was angrily pacing the study room where we were confined like a tiger in a zoo.

"The worst?" asked Jean-Paul with a raised eyebrow. "I think the worst would have been expulsion."

"The only person who was going to get expelled was Black Sheep. And I would have been just fine with that. Actually, I would have been more than fine. I would have been *thrilled!*"

Jean-Paul shook his head and focused on his game of solitaire.

I ignored Sheena and turned to Gray. "Hey . . . thanks for having my back."

"I know they say there's no honor among thieves, but we're in this together, aren't we? I've always got your back. Oh, and checkmate." I glanced down to find several of my chess pieces missing from the table.

"Hey! You cheated!"

Gray grinned and waved my queen at me. "Cheating is encouraged here, remember?"

"He's right," said Antonio as he held up a handful of cards he had taken from Jean-Paul's deck.

Jean-Paul snatched them back with a grin. "I was looking for those!"

Sheena watched us, her hands firmly on her hips. "So you're all okay with being punished for something that was *her* fault?" she cried as she pointed at me. "I don't like being treated like a kindergartener, and I *definitely* don't like taking the fall for something a little brat organized." Sheena approached my desk, her face red with rage. "Gray might have your back, but I'm going to have your hide, little girl."

Sheena was nothing more than a spoiled bully, and I was getting tired of her attitude. I stood up angrily. As soon as I opened my mouth to fire off a retort, I felt that hand on my shoulder again. It was Gray. "Hey, guys?" he asked, trying to calm us down by changing the subject. "What if we use detention to come up with our code names?"

We all nodded at this suggestion and began pulling our chairs into a circle.

As we all knew, code names were important — they had to capture who we were as criminals while still sounding flashy and intimidating.

Antonio suddenly snapped his fingers and turned to Gray. "I have one for you! How about . . . Shocker?"

Gray just shook his head in response.

"The Shocksmith?" offered Jean-Paul.

I jumped up from my seat. "I've got one!" I made a marquee gesture with my hands as if unveiling a grand title. "Power Failure," I said, and I looked expectantly at Gray.

"Failure? I don't think so." Gray was unimpressed. "Sorry, mates. Nothing has that crackle that I'm looking for." Suddenly his eyes widened and he leaped up. "That's it! Ready? My code name is . . . *Graham Crackle.*"

I burst into laughter, and Jean-Paul soon joined in. "Dude, really?" I asked Gray.

"No one's going to take us seriously as criminals if we have *puns* for names," Jean-Paul said.

"Yeah, and he'll sound like an after-school snack," I added, wiping tears from my eyes as I collected myself.

"I could do with a snack myself," said Sheena, who was eyeing a vending machine full of candy bars and bags of chips. She flexed her fingers, and we all stared at her.

Her nails were unlike anything I had seen before. They were long and sharp—*dangerously* sharp. They looked almost claw-like as she ran them along the glass exterior of the vending machine.

"Like my new nail extensions?" she asked, noticing our stares. "They're *très chic* . . . and *très sharp.*"

Sheena ran her index finger in a circle along the glass, cutting out a perfect hole. She reached inside and began taking out snacks one by one as the rest of us looked on, impressed. I did not want to admit that Sheena was becoming a talented criminal, but I was starting to realize that maybe she had potential.

"I live to shop, but I take what I want." Sheena spun on her heel to turn to us with a dramatic flourish. "You can call me . . . Miss Take.*"

Now all four of us burst out laughing. I snickered loudly as Sheena stomped her foot angrily in front of me. "What?" she said.

"Seriously? Say it again. That code name would be a big *mistake.*"

Everyone laughed even louder, and Sheena growled angrily. Her eyes flashed with anger, and everyone quickly went silent—except for me.

I was still giggling when Sheena lunged at me, her nails extended.

I jumped back as Jean-Paul and Antonio managed to

stop her before she reached me. They each grabbed one of her arms. "Easy, Sheena! You'll get us all expelled!" cried Gray as he stepped in between us.

A smile slowly spread across my face as something occurred to me. I had an idea for how to deal with Sheena . . . something VILE Academy would actually encourage.

"Maybe we should settle this thief to thief," I said.

"A competition?" Sheena was intrigued, just as I knew she would be.

"If I win, you get off my back for good. If you win, I'll be your personal slave for a week."

"Month," she countered.

I shrugged. "Make it a year. I don't plan on losing."

I turned to the others. "Empty out your pockets. We need coins." As they did so, I explained the rules to Sheena. "Lucky dozen. We each get six coins, and the first to snatch all of the other person's coins from their pockets wins the game."

Gray handed out the sets of coins. "May the slickest fingers win."

Sheena and I circled each other like boxers in a fighting ring. This was not your typical pickpocketing challenge. Even though I was sure I was the better thief, I knew that Sheena was not to be taken lightly.

Sheena leaped toward me, and I quickly sidestepped

her, using the opportunity to slide my hand into her pocket. My hand came away with a coin. "That's one for Black Sheep!" said Gray, who was keeping score.

Sheena wasted no time in coming in for a second attack. She was quick on her feet, but, for once, my smaller size worked to my advantage. I dodged the attack as her claws sliced toward my pocket, coming away with a second coin from hers. "Two for Black Sheep."

She was getting frustrated, and I knew it. Her frantic lunges were becoming sloppier. Sheena took a few steps back and then vaulted into a series of handsprings, hurling herself toward me like an enraged gymnast. I had to suppress a smile as she approached. Her movements were careless and disorganized. It was just the opportunity I needed.

As Sheena moved past me, she held up her hand with a triumphant cry. Then she opened her palm to reveal— not a coin, but a ball of lint. "Lint? Help yourself!" I told her as I opened my own hand to show her another *three* coins I had taken from her pocket.

"Five to zero, Black Sheep. One more point and Black Sheep wins." Gray sounded impressed.

Sheena ran at me with everything she had. I knew I could dodge the attack, but I didn't take into account the razor-sharp nails she extended in front of her, glistening like knives. I tried to evade her just a moment too late.

I felt a sharp pain sear across my leg as her nails dug into me. Sheena stepped away, laughing as all my coins tumbled from the pocket she had ripped. I clutched my leg and hazily heard Gray asking if I was okay. I ignored him. Rage was beginning to bubble up inside me.

"FOUL!" I yelled at Sheena. My face had turned bright red with fury. Now it was my turn to lose control, and I jumped toward her.

I slammed into Sheena, blood pulsing in my ears. I was no longer thinking rationally. All I knew was that I was angry — *very* angry.

The two of us tumbled across the floor. We were a jumbled mess of kicking and scratching limbs as we each tried to get the best of the other. Though Sheena was older and bigger than me, I didn't let that scare me. I fought back as hard and fast as I could.

Suddenly, I felt a strong set of arms on my shoulders, pulling me back. Jean-Paul was easing me off Sheena, while Antonio was doing the same to her.

But Sheena was not about to let the fight end that easily. "I'm going to put you out to pasture, little lamb!" she snarled as she struggled against the hold of her classmates.

"Easy there, tigress," Gray said between clenched teeth as he helped drag Sheena off.

Sheena suddenly went silent and tilted her head toward him with a grin.

"What?" asked Gray, confused.

"That's it. That's my code name. From now on, I'm . . . *Tigress*." We all went silent then . . . It *was* a good code name for her.

SHEENA HAD FOUND HER PERFECT CODE NAME, AND after that, it didn't take long for everyone else to find their own.

Gray dropped Graham and became Crackle, the operative who exceled at the manipulation of electricity.

Jean-Paul wanted to be *Le Chèvre*. It was a perfect fit, as it was French for "The Goat," and he was a criminal able to climb any heights with ease, just like a mountain goat.

And Jean-Paul's best friend, Antonio, became *El Topo*, which meant "The Mole" in Spanish. While Le Chèvre was master of the high ground, El Topo mastered the low. If you needed a criminal who could dig a network of tunnels in no time at all, El Topo was your guy.

The quiet student who had fought Sheena in Coach Brunt's class came up with not just a code name but a whole new look as well. He began wearing the face paint and outfit of a mime, complete with a striped shirt and

French beret. We all thought it was strange, but then again, he was a strange guy.

To get us to start calling him by his code name, one afternoon he pointed repeatedly to himself, then mimed a huge explosion going off. "Mime . . . Bomb?" I guessed. He nodded enthusiastically, and I laughed. "Okay. Mime Bomb it is." None of us was sure what Mime Bomb's criminal specialty was, but he seemed confident and happy with his new-and-improved identity. Besides, we all thought he was such an oddball that none of us thought to ask.

After everyone in our class had settled on their new names, they turned to me. "And what about you, Black Sheep?" Le Chèvre asked. The thought of being called something else had never once crossed my mind. I was Black Sheep. So I told them what I had told Gray earlier in the school year. "I am Black Sheep. Always have been. Always will be."

CHAPTER 6

I N THE BLINK OF AN EYE, THE SCHOOL YEAR WAS almost over. Time had flown by, and we formed bonds in that year that I thought would never be broken. Jean-Paul and Antonio, who now went exclusively by Le Chèvre and El Topo, were rarely ever seen without each other. Gray was like a big brother to me. He never missed an opportunity to study with me and would often come to me for sleight-of-hand tips.

As the weeks went by, I watched my classmates develop and improve their techniques. They weren't just goofy wannabe criminals anymore. VILE Academy was successfully molding us into something else — something *greater*. Each of us was shaping up to be an expert criminal in our own right.

After we had chosen our code names, we started acquiring our own caper outfits — clothes that we would wear during missions out in the field. I had gotten my very own stealth suit. It was a pitch-black jumpsuit that felt cool and slick against my skin. Brunt told me that it would allow me to slip into even the highest-security places with ease, a perfect camouflage against the night sky. I felt incredible in it, like I could steal the *Mona Lisa* at a moment's notice. I didn't yet know what the others had chosen for their caper outfits, but I had a feeling I would soon find out.

And then there was Player, my friend throughout all of it. I called him from my rooftop hideout whenever I could, very careful not to be spotted or overheard. I would excitedly tell him about what had happened that week . . . though I always kept the details of my lessons and classes a secret. I still hadn't told him that I went to a school for criminals. After all, I had no idea how he would react to hearing news like that—what with his white-hat hackers' code to do only good and all that.

Instead, I would try to get him to tell me about the outside world as much as I could. He'd described his life in Canada in great detail, from the friendly people to the bitter cold that would arrive in the wintertime. His family didn't have a lot of money to travel, but in his room with all his computers, he could see the entire world in his own unique way.

"Of course I want to see the world!" Player said enthusiastically when I asked him about it one day. "I totally want to travel all over, just like you do."

"Really?" I asked, excited that someone else shared my interest. "Where in the world do you want to go?"

"Well . . . there are these totally awesome gaming cafés in Japan. Or I'd go to the video-game tournaments in South Korea! Or the arcades in —"

"I'm sensing a theme here, Player," I told him with a smile.

"Okay, so I like gaming," he admitted. "But I still want to fill up my passport with stamps one day."

I was hiding on the rooftop, my makeshift grappling hook by my side. It was a beautiful spring night. A light breeze rippled through the palm trees as stars lit up the sky over the water.

"All I have to do," I told Player, "is pass my final exams tomorrow. And then, boom! Graduation day."

"I know you can do it!"

"I appreciate your faith in me," I said, still smiling at his enthusiasm. "But these exams aren't going to be easy. They're going to test us like never before."

"I know exactly what you mean. My mom once came up with the craziest algebra test. I wasn't even allowed to use a calculator!"

"Yeah . . . this is something like that."

I'm ready, I told myself that night as I tried to sleep. I was the best thief on the island. Whatever tests the faculty had cooked up for us, I could handle them.

THE FIRST EXAM WAS DR. BELLUM'S. I WALKED INTO class to see a familiar sight—a massive laser grid spanning the entirety of the room. Murmurs swept through the class as we took in the red lasers that crisscrossed in every direction imaginable. Some of them were even rotating.

Gray looked proud as he surveyed the scene.

"Looks like Bellum is putting your invention to good use," I told him. He grinned sheepishly.

"When you are in the field," said Dr. Bellum, "you may encounter a laser security grid, just like this one. For your final exam, you'll have to get through this laser course without touching any of them. Get through the grid, and pick up one of the satchels at the end of the room without being detected by the security alarms. Remember, science and smart thinking are your true friends. Now . . . go!"

Le Chèvre was up first. He looked out at the grid of lasers with a bored expression on his face. He then leaped up and across to the walls, narrowly avoiding the lasers in his path, before springing up toward the ceiling vent. He removed the metal vent from its frame, then crawled up into the air shaft.

"Is he allowed to do that?" Gray asked, amused.

Le Chèvre disappeared completely from view, but we all heard him making his way above the room, the ceiling shaking as he went. Moments later, a ceiling tile at the far end of the room was lifted out of place, and Le Chèvre very calmly dropped down from above. He dusted himself off and claimed his satchel.

Sheena was next. *It's Tigress now,* I reminded myself with an eye roll as I looked over at her. Tigress decided to do things differently and put her gymnastics skills to good use. For once her handsprings weren't just for show—she leaped through the lasers, doing a rolling fall in between two, then a series of somersaults through others. While it was quite a ridiculous sight to see, she made it through the course with ease and avoided every laser.

"Black Sheep! You're up!" Bellum barked. I stepped forward, lightly brushing past Tigress as she returned to her seat. My hand came away with a small compact mirror that I knew she always carried in her pocket. I flipped it open. "Hey! That's mine!" Tigress cried angrily as she saw what was in my hand.

"Don't worry, you can have it back in a minute. It's not really my style," I told her.

I moved straight toward the first set of lasers. Out of the corner of my eye, I saw Bellum lean forward, watching closely to see what I would do next.

I carefully held the mirror out and directly into the

path of the first laser. The compact mirror reflected the laser away from me, confusing the alarm sensors. I made my way forward through the grid, quickly moving the mirror around me to redirect each of the lasers as I went. *This sure beats an algebra test,* I thought.

In a flash, I was through the grid and grabbed one of the waiting satchels. "Black Sheep passes, *and* gets extra credit for a successful theft," Bellum announced. Tigress scowled angrily as I tossed the compact back to her, but I heard Gray clapping from across the room and couldn't hide my grin. Gray was next. He looked at the lasers blocking his path. Instead of taking a step forward into the grid, he took out a pen from his pocket and flung it in the direction of a control panel on the side of the wall. It buried itself into the electric wiring. The panel sparked and smoked and burst into flames. The lasers powered down and disappeared completely. Vlad and Boris spotted the fire from the hallway and quickly rushed to grab a fire extinguisher.

Gray walked casually across the room and picked up a satchel. Dr. Bellum, of course, was thrilled with this result. "Excellent!" she cried. "Most excellent!"

One down, four to go. So far, the exams were off to a great start.

AN HOUR LATER, WE WERE GATHERED IN COACH BRUNT'S gymnasium. "Well, mates, this ought to be good," Gray said as we entered the gym. I nodded in agreement.

Before us was what looked like a boxing ring. It was positioned in the center of the gymnasium, with thick ropes strung across the sides and padded poles in each corner.

Coach Brunt walked out to the front of the gym with big, booming footsteps. "Today we'll see how much you've learned this year. So get ready to impress me." I heard someone gulp loudly behind me. "When you're out in the field, you'll have to evade all sorts of authorities, from your everyday police officers to international crime-fighting organizations like Interpol." Coach Brunt's expression darkened. "Remember, VILE operatives do *not*, under any circumstances, get caught. We are a shadow organization, and we aim to keep it that way. Do I make myself clear?"

We all nodded. Coach Brunt seemed satisfied by this. "Playing the role of the authorities today will be a few *friends* of mine. They are brought to you by Dr. Bellum."

Coach Brunt pulled a remote control out of her pocket and punched a few buttons with her large fingers. Seconds later, a whirring noise began to sound from behind us. Sheena yelped in surprise, and I followed her line of sight.

Filing one by one into the gymnasium were gangly, human-shaped drones that were rolling toward us. They looked like orange crash-test dummies that had been converted into machines. These drones had the high-tech mechanics of Dr. Bellum but seemed to operate with the kind of brute force that we had all come to know Coach Brunt for. They rolled along on wheels as their metallic arms swung back and forth at their sides. I grinned, feeling excited about what was to come.

"Today, each of you will be thieves on the run from authorities. These drones—I like to call 'em *robobuddies* —are programmed to try to apprehend you at any cost. You must evade them and keep them busy until the timer sounds. Use your self-defense training. If they catch you, it's game over."

"Hmph! This will be *way* too easy," said Tigress. She flexed her claws as she watched the robots with narrowed eyes.

"You can use whatever skills you have at your disposal. But remember your lessons above all else—that will be what saves your hide. Who wants to go first?" Tigress's hand shot up in the air. "All right, Tigress. Let's find out if you've earned that code name. Your time starts . . . now!"

Brunt pressed a button on the remote. The drone in the ring looked up, suddenly alert. It was strange to see such lifelike reactions from what looked like a silly crash-test dummy.

"Stop! Thief!" the drone yelled in a digital voice that sounded suspiciously like Boris's.

It took off after Tigress with its bulky arms outstretched. The drone was much faster than I had anticipated, and Tigress seemed to be thinking the same thing. She tried to leap into her typical series of handsprings to get away, but the drone managed to grab on to her wrist before she could move out of its way. While Tigress was restrained, the drone took out a set of handcuffs.

"Is she really going to fail?" I heard Le Chèvre ask aloud next to me. I wondered the same thing.

As if in answer to our question, Tigress kicked up her feet, freeing her wrist from the drone's grasp and managing to leap backwards before she was handcuffed. She looked every bit like an angry feline. I should have known she would have a trick or two up her sleeve.

The drone whirled around to face her once more, but Tigress was faster this time. She swiped at it with her claws, and the drone staggered back. There were long claw marks across the drone's chest where she had struck it. The timer sounded with a loud *beep!*

Tigress strutted back to join us, a proud look on her face.

"Next up . . . El Topo!"

Le Chèvre clapped a hand to El Topo's shoulder as he walked up to the ring. "You can do it, *mon ami.*"

El Topo's hands caught my eye, and I saw that he was wearing thick metal gloves with pointed fingertips. *Those gloves are meant for digging,* I realized. *They must be part of his new caper outfit.*

"How will those help him? It's not like he can tunnel out of the ring," Gray said. He had also taken note of El Topo's newest accessory.

"You underestimate him," Le Chèvre told Gray confidently.

El Topo easily sidestepped the drone's attempts to restrain him while it yelled, "Stop! Thief!" over and over again. Then with one swift strike of his metal-plated hand, El Topo sent the drone flying backwards. It landed on its back and was unable to get up, like a turtle stuck on its shell. Dr. Bellum had done a masterful job of designing the drones, but they were not built to withstand such a blow. The timer rang, and Brunt nodded approvingly.

"Not bad, not bad," Brunt said as she dragged the damaged drone out of the ring with one muscular hand.

"I thought we were just supposed to avoid the drones, not attack them!" I said to Gray as El Topo rejoined us.

"It got the job done, didn't it?" Gray replied with a shrug.

It was my turn next.

I took my spot in the ring and immediately realized how small I was compared to my opponent. "Uhh . . . hey, there," I said as the drone took its spot opposite me in the ring.

I could see Brunt watching closely from the other side of the gym. She gave me a reassuring nod, and I winked at her in response. I was getting fired up. I couldn't wait to show her just how ready I was to be out in the field as a VILE operative.

The buzzer sounded, and the drone rushed toward me. This one yelled in Boris's voice, "You are under arrest! Stop in the name of the law!"

With each lunge and swing of the drone's arms, I ducked and ran, moving in a swerving pattern across the ring. The drone seemed to become more and more frantic with each passing minute that it failed to catch me. It zoomed toward me with a surprising amount of force.

I actually laughed as I ducked and darted, avoiding the drone's attempts to restrain me. I jumped up on top of the rope surrounding the ring, walking across it like a tightrope walker, safely out of reach of the flailing drone.

BZZZT!

The timer sounded loudly, and I heard Coach Brunt clap enthusiastically. "That's how it's done, Lambkins!"

THAT AFTERNOON, WE WALKED INTO COUNTESS CLEO'S classroom to find her standing next to a beautiful oil painting. The painting was of a young woman staring back at the viewer with a mysterious expression on her face. I recognized it immediately as *Girl with a Pearl Earring* by the Dutch painter Johannes Vermeer. It was one of the most famous paintings in the world, and I was taken aback by its beauty. For a moment, I forgot all about the exam. If the painting was a fake, it was a very good one.

El Topo said aloud what we were all wondering. "That is a forgery, yes? That cannot possibly be the real *Girl with a Pearl Earring*?"

Then again, we were on Vile Island at a school for thieves. Anything was possible.

Cleo turned to us and gestured for silence. "Today, for your final exam . . . you will be working in teams."

The entire class groaned loudly. A group project? I *hated* those. How was I supposed to stand out and prove I was the best thief here if I had to work with others?

Cleo clapped her hands for silence. "This will be a mock art heist. You will each play a different role in stealing this painting here. I will provide you with information about a fake museum that we will pretend it is being shown in, as well as the surrounding area. You must decide as a team how you would get the painting out of the museum, replace it with a forgery, and successfully get it to Vile Island. I will also be throwing in, shall we say . . . *obstacles,* as you go."

"What kind of obstacles?" I asked.

Countess Cleo flashed an irritated look in my direction. "Telling you would spoil the surprise. I had hoped that after a year in my class, you would have learned to be less disruptive, Black Sheep." I winced as Tigress snickered loudly behind me. Countess Cleo pressed on. "It is important that you think on your feet as operatives and work as a team if you are to steal such rare and beautiful goods as this one. There will be a prize for the team that is able to pull off their heist with the most creativity, skill, and speed."

Countess Cleo split us into groups. I was with Gray, Le Chèvre, Tigress, and Mime Bomb. I was sure that Countess Cleo had purposefully paired me with Tigress just to make my life difficult. And I had no doubt that Tigress felt the same way about me.

"All right, you two," Gray said, anticipating trouble, "let's just ace this and get it over with."

"Don't look at me," Tigress snapped. "I'll be on my best behavior. Just make sure little Miss Disruptive doesn't cost us any points."

Countess Cleo passed out paper packets to each group containing maps of the museum for our make-believe heist. They had everything we needed to know to plot out our big caper.

Sheena tried to shut down any suggestion I made, but a plan soon began to fall into place, and eventually we managed to design a caper that I knew Countess Cleo would approve of.

For our mock heist, Tigress insisted on being the one to steal the painting, claiming her skills as a cat burglar made her the ideal thief to get the bounty. Gray would take care of shutting down the alarms by disabling the electricity. Le Chèvre would escape with the painting over the rooftops, avoiding any authorities on the streets below. I would pick the pocket of the security guard and take his keycard, allowing me to switch out the surveillance tapes. There was just one missing link in the chain . . .

"What about Mime Bomb?" I finally asked.

"Maybe he can distract the police with a game of charades," Tigress said.

"Let's be serious. What *can* he do?"

The group was silent as we pondered this. I felt a pair of eyes on me and turned to see Mime Bomb grinning.

He mimed looking around, then pointed repeatedly to his ears.

"Eyes and ears?" I asked.

"Oh, great, this is just what we need during our *final exam*," Tigress groaned.

Mime Bomb gestured to the gathered students and once again pointed to his eyes, then his ears. Finally I understood.

"He's saying he can see and hear everything. The

lookout! Mime Bomb can be our eyes and ears on the museum floor." Mime Bomb jumped up and down and clapped his hands at this, then gave me a thumbs-up. Clearly, I had gotten it right, and we decided that Mime Bomb would signal to us with flashlights from his lookout spot if anything went wrong.

"Glad that's settled," Gray said dryly.

True to her word, Countess Cleo added several obstacles to make things more interesting in our imaginary heist. When she told us the "authorities" had followed us to our getaway train, I examined the maps and redirected us to a nearby airfield. Moments later, Cleo announced that there was now a torrential downpour that threatened to ruin the priceless painting we were stealing, so I found an underground network of tunnels that we could carry the painting through, keeping it both dry and hidden. "El Topo would be proud of this idea," Le Chèvre said with a smile when I explained the solution.

Despite the fact that we were in the middle of an exam, I was having a lot of fun. The fake caper felt more like an elaborate game to me—and it was a game that I wanted to *win*.

When Countess Cleo announced the winning group at the end of the exam, we were thrilled to hear our names. Then she passed out dainty jeweled letter openers to each member of our group.

"A letter opener? Uh . . . thank you, Countess Cleo." Gray looked over his gift with a confused expression on his face.

Cleo huffed. "These are not just any letter openers. These are some of the best lockpicks in the world. *And* the most fashionable."

"Sweet!" exclaimed Tigress, turning her lockpick so it glittered in the light.

Cleo was about to hand me my own lockpick when she suddenly changed her mind and put it away. "For you, Black Sheep, I have something different." I perked up, awaiting my prize. *I must be getting something special for solving all those obstacles,* I thought. But to my dismay, she handed me a small book. I read the title: *"Miss Etiquette . . . All Manner of Manners for Modern Living?"* I frowned.

"May it do you good, Black Sheep."

I sighed and pocketed the book. *Maybe I can use it if I ever need to start a fire,* I thought.

We had no idea what to expect going into Professor Maelstrom's exam. His classes during the school year had been filled with both unpredictable weirdness and moments of brilliance.

In the weeks leading up to our exams, we studied and practiced in each and every subject, yet when it came to Maelstrom's class, we found that there was little we could do to prepare. How do you prepare for the unexpected?

As I walked into his classroom, I saw dozens of pedestals arranged in neat rows across the floor. Resting on top of the pedestals were objects of all shapes and sizes. On top of one was a large black volcanic rock; another had a tiny pearl. Yet another had a gold watch; on a fourth was a fountain pen. No two were alike.

We filed slowly into the room. I tried my best to figure out what Maelstrom had in store for us. Were we meant to steal the items? Forge copies of them?

Maelstrom looked gleeful as he sat at his desk. "During your first class," Maelstrom began slowly, "I taught you about the bait and switch. The bait and switch, as you know, works only when an object is switched with something of equal weight and size."

He stood up and gestured toward the pedestals. "Each object here has an equal. When I say 'Go,' you are to grab an object and switch it with the object that matches it in weight. The pedestals are outfitted with sensors. If you're wrong—*BZZZT!* I'm afraid you'll be in for quite a *shock!*" He grinned wickedly. "Better grab the right one before someone else takes it!"

"You mean we're not going one at a time?" I asked.

"Of course not! Where would be the fun in that?"

I looked across at my classmates. They each looked as though they were warming up for a race. Tigress was ready to pounce. Even Mime Bomb was flexing his hands.

As for me, I examined the objects on the pedestals as quickly as I could. If I could immediately locate two objects that matched, then I could switch them as fast as possible before others were taken.

The problem was, all the objects looked so different that it was difficult to tell what the correct pairs were. I looked at a snow globe with a miniature Eiffel Tower inside. The more closely I examined it, the more it looked to be the same size as one of my Russian nesting dolls —and I knew the exact weight and feel of that for sure.

I quickly looked around for the object that matched it in weight, and my eyes landed on a leather-bound notebook. I took out the *Miss Etiquette* book that Cleo had given me and held it in my hand. It felt about the same weight as my Russian nesting doll, and the notebook on the pedestal and Cleo's book looked practically identical.

Maelstrom set off a foghorn that was so loud, it shook the walls of the classroom. And then we were off.

There was a mad dash to grab the objects from their pedestals. No one had thought to go after the snow globe, and I grabbed it quickly.

I turned to take the notebook from its resting place,

but a clawed hand swiped it from right in front of me. I turned around to see Tigress waving the notebook at me.

"Looking for this, little girl?"

Tigress removed a candlestick from a pedestal and put the notebook down in its place. *Those aren't the same,* I thought. I was right.

"Aahh!" Tigress shrieked, and jumped back as a loud buzzer sounded from the pedestal, followed by the crackling sound of an electric shock. Her blond hair stood on end.

As she wobbled and tried to regain balance, I used her moment of distraction to grab the notebook. "Thanks for this!" I said with a smile.

I hurriedly replaced the snow globe with the notebook, jumping back as quickly as I could — just in case. To my relief, the pedestal made a satisfying *ping!* sound, and a light on the platform glowed a soft blue.

"Nice going, Black Sheep!" Gray said to me with a grin. The pedestal he was standing next to was also glowing blue. He had guessed right and switched the black rock with a baseball glove.

One by one, the pedestals glowed blue as the students paired the objects correctly. Even though I was hoping she would fail, Tigress eventually found the right switch to make after replacing a tiny pearl with one of Maelstrom's cufflinks.

Professor Maelstrom clapped slowly. "Not bad, not bad . . ." he said. The doors opened, and Vlad and Boris entered, carrying platters of wriggling worms.

"Ugh! Disgusting!" Tigress said as she plugged her nose. Many of the other students were doing the same.

"Don't you remember? You successfully made the switch; now have some bait!" Maelstrom cackled.

I rolled my eyes. "This joke is getting old . . ."

FINALLY, IT WAS TIME FOR THE LAST EXAM.

We were seated in Shadowsan's classroom, our bare feet crossed on our mats. After the craziness of the last four exams, I knew I could handle anything Shadowsan had planned.

"What do you think it'll be this time?" El Topo asked. He was looking around for any sign of a complicated setup like the ones we had seen in the other classrooms.

As far as I could tell, everything seemed to be normal.

At the head of the room, Shadowsan looked up from a clipboard with a sour expression. "For the first exam, I call Tigress."

"I got this," Tigress said haughtily. She had added to her caper outfit a pair of goggles that rested on top of her head and brought out her catlike features. She pulled the goggles down over her eyes as she walked up to join Shadowsan, making a loud click-clacking sound on the floor. Everyone's eyes went to her feet. While the rest of us had removed our shoes, Tigress was sporting a pair of high heels—also a new addition to her getup. They had to have been at least three inches tall. She was breaking classroom rules and not even trying to hide it.

"That'll cost her," I murmured to Gray.

I pretended not to notice when she stopped to crush an origami sheep beneath her heel as she went.

"Somewhere in my coat," said Shadowsan as he put on a black trench coat, "is a single dollar bill. The coat has many pockets." He gave each of us a long look, though I felt as though the gaze he gave me was longer than anyone else's. "Locate the target, and acquire it—if you can." He took out a timer and placed it on the desk. "You have two minutes."

I heard Gray guffaw next to me. "Two whole minutes? *If* she can?"

The test was so simple. Compared to the exams we had just gone through, it almost seemed *too* simple. Where were the robots or the lasers? We really just had to steal a dollar bill from a trench coat?

Shadowsan started the timer.

Tigress was up for the challenge. She prowled around Shadowsan like a cat circling its prey. In a flash, she lunged toward Shadowsan. With barely any movement at all, Shadowsan caught Tigress's wrist in his hand before she could reach his coat. Tigress hissed and pulled back, getting ready to try again.

Once more she pounced toward Shadowsan, and once more he caught her wrist before she could steal from his coat. I could tell that Tigress was getting frustrated. I leaned forward in my seat and noticed that my classmates were all doing the same. *Will Tigress lose her cool?* I wondered.

Tigress lunged forward a third time—but it was a fake-out! She avoided Shadowsan's grasp. Suddenly, Tigress reached toward the nearby Japanese zen garden that was filled to the brim with sand. Before Shadowsan realized what she was about to do, Tigress reached down and grabbed a fistful of sand. With a wicked smile, she flung the sand straight toward Shadowsan's face. I heard Gray gasp as Shadowsan stumbled backwards, his hands clutching his eyes. Tigress pounced on her opportunity. Her long claws sliced through the air as she swiped toward the instructor's coat.

A heavy silence filled the room. For a split second, everything seemed frozen in time.

And then Shadowsan's coat fell to the floor in ribbons, shredded by Tigress's claws.

Tigress casually walked over to the strips of the coat

and picked up the dollar bill from among the remains. "Looking for this?" she asked Shadowsan with a victorious smile.

I turned to Gray. "There's no way Shadowsan will pass her. He's got to call foul." Gray nodded in agreement.

"Unorthodox technique," said Shadowsan, his expression souring as he wiped grains of sand from his face. I held back a smile, knowing he would announce her failure at any moment. But to my surprise, Shadowsan bowed to Tigress. "But excellent results."

My jaw dropped, and I turned to Gray in outrage. "No way! Shadowsan's totally playing favorites!"

"Black Sheep, you are up next," came Shadowsan's voice from the front of the room. I took a deep breath to calm myself down and walked up to face him. *I'll show him.*

Shadowsan put on another trench coat. This one was undamaged by Tigress. Once again, he started the timer.

I took another deep breath, centering myself. There was no way I was going to be able to do this successfully if I let my anger get in the way. I focused on my training and did my best to clear my mind. This was my chance to prove that I wasn't a reckless child anymore — I was a skilled thief, and I was ready to become a graduate of VILE Academy.

Calmly and nimbly, I made a grab for his coat. I was

able to slip my hand into one of the pockets on my first try, dodging Shadowsan's grabs, but my hand came out empty. *That's okay,* I thought, keeping a mental note of which pocket didn't have the dollar bill in it.

I made a second pass at the coat, but this time Shadowsan caught my arm. Even as I was flung backwards, I managed to slide my other hand into one of the pockets. Again I came up empty.

Don't lose your cool, don't lose your cool, I told myself. I could feel the rest of the class watching me. From the corner of my eye, I saw Gray nodding encouragingly. *Focus,* I told myself.

Over and over again, I tried to find the dollar without success. I could hear the ticking of the timer as I lunged and dove toward Shadowsan. It seemed to get louder and louder with each passing minute. I must have reached into a dozen pockets or more, and each time my hand came back empty. With each lunge I made, Shadowsan became more aggressive in his defense. He started by simply avoiding my attempts at reaching toward the coat, but soon he was advancing toward me, forcing me backwards. I almost stumbled over my own feet as he came at me, managing to catch myself only at the last second.

BEEP!

The timer rang out.

I froze in place. I couldn't believe I had failed

—there was no way! I stared at Shadowsan, who simply looked back at me with a cold expression that was filled with . . . disappointment? Hatred? It was not easy to read, but it was definitely not good. "Your time is up, Black Sheep. Take your seat."

I forced my legs to walk slowly back to my seat, feeling numb. I tried to ignore the whispers from the other students, but the sound of Tigress's giggles rang loudly in my ears.

"I HIT EVERY POCKET," I TOLD GRAY AS WE WALKED together through the halls hours later. I had been the only one to fail Shadowsan's exam and was feeling shaken. "I *know* I hit every pocket! If there was a dollar in there, I couldn't find it." Even though I aced every other exam, I was crushed by my performance in Shadowsan's class.

"So you choked a little," Gray said cheerfully. "It was probably just nerves. Don't worry about it. There's no way that could affect your grade. You're the best pickpocket in our class. Totally in a league of your own."

"You think so?"

Gray patted his heart. "I know so."

I gave him a grateful smile, feeling better by the second.

A familiar click-clacking sound came toward me from down the hall, and soon Tigress was at our side.

"You might want to pick a different pair of shoes if you don't want to get caught when you're a thief," I told her. "The police will hear you coming a mile away."

"Actually, it turns out I don't need to sacrifice fashion for the job. These shoes are a mean weapon," she said, swinging her foot around in a high arc that came toward me as fast as lightning. I didn't move. There was a loud *crunch* as her sharp heel burrowed into the wall a few inches from my head.

"See?" Tigress said as she pulled her foot back. "It's the *authorities* who should be worried about *me*."

"Whatever you say, *Sheena*," I said with a snicker, purposefully using her real name just to annoy her.

"It's *Tigress* now, little Lambkins."

I ignored her attempts to make me angry. "Remember what Coach Brunt said? You have to *earn* your code name."

"I think I've earned it. I aced all my exams . . . which is more than you can say. "

Gray stepped in front of Tigress. "She's still a better thief than you."

"She's not better than me, and she never will be."

"Enough!" I yelled. "I'm a better thief than you, and you know it! That's why you've always hated me!"

I knew I was right, but Tigress didn't become angry like I thought she would. "If you're so much better than me, then how come I aced Shadowsan's exam and you failed?" she whispered in my ear and walked off before I could respond.

DOWN THE HALL, STUDENTS WERE SHOUTING AND cheering. They were all gathered next to a large electronic bulletin board. As I approached, I saw Le Chèvre and El Topo, and they beckoned us over. "Results are in!" El Topo said excitedly as Gray and I rushed to join them.

I jumped up and down, trying to peer over the heads of the taller students who were high-fiving each other and exchanging congratulations. Le Chèvre and El Topo hugged each other. "Upward and downward, *mi amigo!*" El Topo said with a grin as he clapped his friend on the shoulder.

Gray pushed his way through the crowd to the front. He quickly turned away from me, frowning. "Didn't you pass . . . ?" I asked, confused. There was no way Gray had failed after he had done so well in all his classes.

"I passed," he said, clearly trying to hide his sadness. "But . . ."

Could it be that Gray had passed . . . *but I hadn't?*

I fought my way through the crowd and looked up at the results. Next to my name was a *big red X*.

I fought back tears, trying not to feel the full weight of my shattered dreams. All around me I could hear the sounds of celebrating as my classmates whooped and hollered.

Gray looked as though he was trying to think of something to say to me when Tigress approached him. She took him by the elbow, leading him away. "Come on, Crackle. Sit at the big kids' table with us." He looked back at me, as if for permission, and I nodded at him. "Go on, Gray," I said with forced cheerfulness. "I'll be fine."

My heart hurt as I watched them leave without me. Everything I had worked for, everything I had planned for . . . it had all been for nothing.

CHAPTER 7

I CREPT AWAY TO THE ROOFTOP AND PULLED OUT MY cellphone. Gray was celebrating with the rest of the soon-to-be graduates, and I didn't want to bring him down with my disappointment. Luckily there was someone else who always knew how to help.

"Black Sheep?"

"Hey, Player."

"Are you okay? What's wrong?" As usual, Player could read the emotions in my voice.

"I failed one of my exams. And now . . . now I'm going to have to repeat the program." My voice cracked as I said it. I had been trying to deny the reality of my situation, but it was finally hitting me. *I had failed.*

"That's . . . that's crazy! You've worked so hard for this!" Player sounded shocked. He didn't know the truth about VILE Academy because I always kept the details of my schooling secret, but even so, he knew how much this meant to me.

"I know! But it's done," I said.

"Can't you, I don't know, talk to your professor or something? What if they let you have a do-over?"

"I failed. It's not like I can retake—" The gears began spinning wildly in my head. "Player! You're a genius!"

"I know, I know. You could try saying it more often, though."

I smiled the tiniest bit as right then my feelings of disappointment and despair were replaced by determination.

LATER THAT NIGHT, I MADE MY WAY THROUGH THE HALL-ways of VILE Academy. The sun had set hours ago, and the halls looked eerie in the darkness.

I watched from around a corner as Shadowsan left his classroom and closed the door to lock it for the night. I darted behind him, my hand brushing past him in the nimblest of movements.

Shadowsan patted his pockets, reaching inside to find them empty.

"Looking for these?" I asked, dangling his keys in my hand.

"Playing games? Typical," Shadowsan said with annoyance.

"This isn't a game," I said defiantly. "I want a do-over."

Shadowsan took his keys from me, locked the door, and pocketed them. He barely looked at me. "And you will have it," he said. I brightened, feeling hopeful. "Next year. Once you redo your coursework." The disappointment crept back in.

I'm not giving up that easily, I thought as I stepped in front of him, blocking his path. I had worked too hard for this and was not about to accept defeat without a fight. "You're not hearing me," I said firmly. "Put on the coat. I want a do-over *now!*"

Shadowsan stepped around me and began to walk away. He didn't even pause to look at me as he continued down the hallway. "We do not change the rules for other students, and it is my belief that we must stop changing them for you. Good night, Black Sheep."

I felt anger bubbling up inside me like an active volcano.

"The coat was empty, wasn't it?" I yelled before I realized what I was saying.

Shadowsan stopped dead in his tracks. He slowly turned around and walked back toward me. I immediately knew that I had crossed a line — in all my time on the island, I had never seen Shadowsan so angry.

"Are you accusing a VILE instructor of cheating?" His words cut through me like a sword.

I gathered my courage and tried to make my case as

best I could—I *had* to try. "I'm sorry. It's just that I know I'm as good as the other students in my class. Better, even."

I dangled his keys in front of him again. I had stolen them a second time.

Shadowsan furiously snatched them away. "You are unruly, undisciplined, and a prankster. I would strongly urge you to find a way to get those qualities in check, since they seem to be holding you back."

He walked away, leaving me alone in the darkened hallway. I was overcome with anger—not at Shadowsan, but at myself. *What if he's right?* What if I had ruined my chances of getting off the island? There was no one else to blame.

THE GRADUATION CEREMONY WAS IN FULL SWING IN THE assembly hall. I watched through the cracks between the auditorium doors, my knees tucked up close to my chest.

Inside, I could see each of the faculty members lined up on the stage. Next to them, Vlad and Boris were playing "For He's a Jolly Good Fellow" on an accordion and hand cymbals.

Coach Brunt made her way up to the podium and took her place behind the microphone. It was just like orientation, only now the students were moving on from the academy . . . everyone except me.

"Congratulations, graduates," Brunt began. There were celebratory shouts and hollers from the students in the audience. "You have proven yourselves worthy of becoming VILE operatives. From this day forward, you are part of our little family." Brunt's expression suddenly became frighteningly serious. "Do *not* let us down," she said slowly as a few of the graduates shifted nervously in their seats. "Valuable Imports, Lavish Exports . . . soon you will travel across all seven continents in pursuit of these precious goods."

I sighed. Traveling across all seven continents? That was supposed to be *my* destiny.

Next it was Maelstrom's turn to speak. He curled his long, thin fingers around the podium. His beady eyes examined the graduates carefully. "Never forget what you have learned here. You will need to put your skills to good use if you wish to succeed as a career criminal." He stared out into the audience, sending a chill up my spine. "You have done well to join with VILE. I look forward to seeing what you can do in the field. Steal as much as you can, as often and as diabolically as you can."

Cheers followed his speech. *If VILE really wanted to be successful, they would send me out there,* I thought. *I'm the best thief on this island.*

Two days later, I sat out on the beach. I was trying to overcome my sadness so that I could be ready to take on the challenges ahead, but my misery wasn't going anywhere. Even though graduation had come and gone, the feelings of failure hadn't left me.

Right now, at this very moment, the graduates were being given their first assignments as VILE operatives. They would leave the island and steal exotic artifacts in faraway places. And I wasn't going to be a part of it.

There was a ringing coming from my pocket. I took out my phone and saw Player's familiar white-hat icon on the screen. I answered it as quickly as I could, keeping my voice muffled.

"Player! You know the rule! *I call you!*"

"I know, I know! I was just . . . worried about you."

I sighed. It was true that I had been avoiding everyone since exams, and that had included Player.

"I'm sorry."

"So . . . are you really going to repeat the year all over again?"

"I'm not sure yet. I didn't think I had a choice, but I've been thinking . . . maybe it's time to make my *own* choices."

I heard a sound from the rocky outcrop above me and looked up. It was Mime Bomb. He was sitting by himself, staring off into the distance. I quickly hid my phone as fast as I could. *Did he see it?* I wondered. I waved an enthusiastic hello.

"What's shaking, Mime Bomb?" I asked.

He mimed crying, his shoulders rocking in fake heaving sobs. At first I thought he was mocking my sadness, but as his crying intensified, it dawned on me that *he* was sad too.

"Something wrong, Mime Bomb?" I asked.

Nearby, the academy doors opened and the sound of graduates talking to one another drifted toward me.

Tigress, Le Chèvre, and El Topo ran down the steps to the waterfront. They were all wearing their caper outfits now—slick, high-tech clothes that matched their new VILE-operative identities perfectly. I looked down at my student uniform, longing for my black jumpsuit. With everyone else moving on, I might as well have had *failure* stamped across my forehead in this uniform.

Eventually I saw Gray coming down the steps. I turned back to Mime Bomb and pretended to hand him an invisible handkerchief. "Here's a hanky. Keep it," I said, and ran over toward Gray.

"Hey, kid sister," Gray said as I approached.

There was an air of awkwardness between us that was impossible to ignore, but I tried to push past it as best I could.

"Do you . . . uh . . . do you know why Mime Bomb's

so upset?" I asked, trying to avoid talking about graduation.

"Mime Bomb? Oh, he got cut from tonight's mission." I knew Gray must be referring to his first big VILE caper that he had been assigned to, along with his teammates Tigress, El Topo, and Le Chèvre.

"But he graduated!" I said, surprised.

"Not every heist has a role for a silent clown." We both chuckled at that.

"Well . . . I guess this is it." I shuffled my feet awkwardly, unsure of how to say goodbye to my friend. He was about to go off to an exotic place on an exciting heist —the first of many—while I was staying put to redo the school year. "I'm surprised you're still here," I said. Graduation was two days ago, so why were my classmates still on the island? It couldn't have taken them that long to get their assignments.

"Just when you think you're out, Coach Brunt makes you go to a 'mandatory senior seminar' and pulls you back in," Gray explained with a laugh. "We're shipping out tonight."

I didn't laugh with him this time. I could no longer hide the sadness I was feeling in my heart.

Gray was no fool—he saw the change in my expression and leaned down to talk to me. "Look, Black Sheep . . . I know it's going to be torture going through the program all over again. But you're still a kid. You're way ahead of the game. Stay focused. Time will fly. You'll make it off this island way sooner than you think." He ruffled my hair and took off down the steps to join his fellow classmates. *Actually, they're his fellow* operatives *now,* I thought.

Gray's parting words seemed to hang in the air. For the first time in days, I smiled. I wasn't just a kid. I was a great thief, and I could prove it. I *was* going to make it off the island . . . sooner than *everyone* thought.

CHAPTER 8

THAT NIGHT, I SLIPPED OUT OF MY DORM ROOM AS silently as a ninja — just like Shadowsan had taught me. Anyone who looked inside my room would see a sleeping form on my bed. They would have no idea that it was really my globe and some pillows stuck under the blankets.

It was dark, but I knew those halls like the back of my hand. Growing up on the island had its perks, and one of them was that after spending my entire early life here, I knew my way around better than anyone. I had mapped the entire academy years ago out of boredom, but now I was finally putting that knowledge to good use.

I crept quietly through the hallway until I found what I was looking for. It was a storm drain, large enough to crawl through, that would take me out of the academy building and all the way to the far end of the island unseen. I ducked inside and crawled through the drain on my hands and knees. I felt a thick, wet slime underneath my fingers. "Yuck!" I cried aloud, then clapped a hand to my mouth. I continued through the pipe until I came to the grate at the end.

Through the grate I could see the harbor, but to my surprise, there was no boat in sight. When Gray said "shipping out," I had assumed that he and the others would be leaving by boat tonight. *So how are they getting off the island?* I wondered.

My question was answered by the sound of a loud engine starting up. I peered upward through the grate at the end of the storm drain and saw a helicopter waiting on the landing pad past a palm-tree grove. Of course! Why hadn't I thought of the helicopter? It was very high-tech, with a sleek jet-black exterior that almost made it look invisible against the dark night sky. The engine grew louder and the metal blades on top began to spin, faster and faster, until a strong wind was blowing in all directions.

They were about to take off!

I grabbed the grate and pushed with all my might. Finally, it budged and fell open, allowing me to slip out of the storm drain and onto the cliffside.

Something moved in the shadows behind me, and just for a moment, I thought I saw a pale face in the darkness. It was in the rocks a short distance away. I blinked. Mime Bomb? *It couldn't be,* I thought. There was no way he was out here at this time of night. I decided it must be my mind playing tricks on me and returned my focus to the task at hand.

A group of figures approached the helicopter, and I ducked behind a nearby boulder. Tigress, Le Chèvre, El Topo, and Gray were making their way toward the helicopter doors. "School's out, boys," I heard Tigress say. "Time to strut our stuff." I rolled my eyes.

I would have to move fast if I was going to make it onto the helicopter unseen. I found myself wishing even more that I had my caper outfit, something stealthy that would blend into the dark of the night. But there was no use worrying about that. It was now or never. I took a deep breath and ran.

I darted forward across the rocks and onto the helicopter pad. The metal rotors were spinning almost at full speed now, and the resulting gusts of wind practically blew me straight across the landing.

I used all my strength to push forward toward the open door. As fast as I could, I grabbed the sides of the helicopter and pulled myself inside. I then tucked and rolled into the supply area, where I would be hidden from view, and curled up to make myself as small as possible. I hid there until the others climbed into the helicopter one by one. They were talking among themselves as they took their seats. I breathed a quiet sigh of relief. They hadn't seen me.

The doors closed, and there was a strange weightless sensation under my feet as the helicopter lifted into the air. I took deep breaths and smiled as I held my knees tight to my chest.

I was leaving the island! For the first time in my entire life, I was going to see what the outside world was like. I was so excited, I wanted to laugh, to yell and holler. Instead I held my hands to my mouth to keep myself from making any noise.

The minutes passed slowly. I could hear the muffled voices of El Topo and Le Chèvre talking to each other, but the sound of the engine made it impossible to hear what they were saying. I managed to make out the words "gem" and "dig," but I heard nothing that would tell me where it was that we were going.

After a while, I decided to risk shifting my position so that I could see out the window. I was dying to know where we were headed. Outside, I saw the ocean and a hilly, mountainous coastline below us.

Suddenly I felt a buzzing in my pocket, and I nearly shouted in surprise. I hurriedly grabbed my cellphone. I had forgotten I had it. There was the usual white-hat graphic on the screen.

"Player? Now is really not a good time!" I half whispered, half shouted at him. "Don't you remember the rules?"

"I know, I know. I'm not allowed to call you on campus, but now you're not on campus. Are you taking a little field trip?"

"What? How did you know?" Despite the circumstances, I was amazed at how much he was able to figure out just by using the computers he had at his home.

"Remember how I could never hack past the jammers at your school to find out your location?"

"Yeah, that's why you've never known where in the world I was."

"Well, guess what? Your phone suddenly lit up on my dashboard. And according to real time, it looks like you're on your way to—"

"Drop point: Assume your positions!" Vlad commanded loudly over the helicopter intercom.

"I'll have to call you back!" I hung up in a hurry and stashed the phone in my pocket.

Drop point? So the helicopter wasn't going to be landing at all—the operatives were going to *parachute* down to their assigned location! If I was going to really escape the island, I would have to parachute too; otherwise I'd be brought right back.

One by one, each of the helicopter's passengers walked over to a rack and grabbed a parachute pack. Le Chèvre, then El Topo, then Tigress each took a parachute and pulled it on as they would a backpack. Gray was last. To my horror, he took the final parachute and began strapping it on. I gasped as the helicopter's rear door began to open.

Le Chèvre jumped first, with a look of pure joy on his face. He seemed all too thrilled to be jumping out of a helicopter thousands of feet in the air — the highest ground ever. He was followed quickly by El Topo, who seemed less than happy to throw himself into the sky. I thought I heard him muttering something about "belonging on the ground" as he walked toward the open door. Nevertheless, he readied himself and jumped out of the helicopter with ease.

Tigress was next. She hesitated beside the open door, her knees shaking. I found myself wishing I didn't have to hide so that I could make fun of her for being so scared. Luckily Gray was thinking the same thing.

Gray walked up behind her. "What are you waiting for?" he asked. "Cats always land on their feet." Before Tigress could think of something clever to say back, Gray raised a boot and shoved her out the door. She gave a high-pitched screech as she plummeted toward the ground.

Sounds just like a cat, I thought.

It was now or never. "Hey!" I yelled. Gray turned toward me, and his mouth dropped open in surprise. He was shocked and unsure of what to do, which is exactly what I was hoping for. I saw my chance and took it, running straight toward him like a football player.

"Oof!" Gray's breath caught in his chest as I barreled into him. He was sent flying backwards straight out of the helicopter, and I fell with him into the open sky.

I clung tightly to Gray as the two of us fell. Wind rushed past my face, and I was gripped by the cold air.

"Black Sheep?" I heard Gray exclaim above the sound of the roaring wind.

"D-d-d-don't let go!" I told him, my teeth chattering wildly. I was frozen to the bone. I had only my school uniform to shield me from the icy air blowing past me. I had been so focused on escaping the island that I hadn't even thought to find a coat. But despite the cold, I felt warm inside, because I knew Gray wouldn't let me go.

Clouds rushed past us. The distant rocky ground was getting closer and closer by the second.

I tried to ignore the sickening falling sensation in the pit of my stomach. Suddenly, I saw Le Chèvre's parachute open and billow up into a mushroom shape far below us. Soon after, two more opened that I knew must be El Topo's and Tigress's. Then it was our turn. Gray pulled a cord on his parachute pack, and we both felt a sudden jolt as the parachute burst out, catching us.

We floated gently toward the ground. Around us, I could see what looked like ancient ruins, with towers of crumbling stones rising from the ground in the desert landscape.

Gray and I landed a short distance away from the others. As the parachute fell to the ground, he took off the pack and tossed it aside.

Suddenly Gray grabbed me by my arms, which were still frozen stiff from the cold. "Are you out of your mind?" He kept his voice down so the others couldn't hear, but it was filled with shock and concern. Gray looked around to make sure none of the others had seen me and then leaned down toward me angrily. "You just put your life and my entire criminal career at risk!" he cried as loudly as he dared. I tried to walk away, but he pulled me back.

"Relax! I'm the one who stowed away," I told him. "They'll have no reason to blame you."

"What do you think the faculty will do when they find out you decided to tag along on our mission?"

I shrugged. "Who cares? I'll be long gone by then."

"Doing what? Backpacking around the world? You're still a kid! You have no money, no connections . . . How will you eat?"

"I'll steal, obviously!" It seemed simple enough to me. I needed to get off the island, and now I had done that. I could go wherever I wanted, stealing as I went.

"Crackle? Let's move!" Tigress's shrill voice pierced through the ruins.

"Stay here. I mean it," Gray told me sternly. "You can't

mess up our first heist. It's everything we've worked so hard for."

Gray ran off through the ruins and turned onto a narrow stone street.

"Time to crash a caper," I said aloud with a smile.

CHAPTER 9

I WALKED QUICKLY THROUGH THE RUINS IN THE DIRECtion in which I had seen Gray leave a moment earlier. I picked up my pace, not wanting to be lost in a foreign land after dark. I quickly ran past a pile of stone rubble — and gasped.

Before me I recognized the soaring tower of the elaborate oceanfront Hassan II Mosque — iconic to the shimmering skyline of Casablanca, Morocco. I could see the ocean rolling up against the rocky shore, and the city streets aglow in the moonlight, casting a purple hue on the white stone buildings.

Up until now, I had seen sights like this only in my books. Seeing the magnificent North African city up close was more beautiful than I could have possibly imagined.

I'm in Morocco, I thought giddily. *I've made it to the real world.*

I forced myself to look away from the view of the city below and focus on what I had to do. The mission would have to come first. If everything went according to plan, there would be plenty of time for sightseeing later.

I weaved through the ruins, making my way through winding dirt paths. Gray and the others were long gone by the time I made it down to Casablanca. I had been following their path by tracking their footprints, but those soon vanished into the dusty sidewalks. I now had no choice but to try to find the location of the heist on my own, though I didn't have much to go on.

All around me were the sights and sounds of a city —a *real* city. I had never before heard shop owners closing down for the day, or groups of tourists chatting over coffee at street-side cafés. Casablanca was buzzing with life.

As I turned onto an empty side street, my feet ached and my stomach started to grumble. I clasped a hand to my stomach to try to silence it, and in the same moment I spied a bakery ahead. The smell of freshly baked bread drifted toward me, causing my mouth to water.

Gray won't be the only one pulling his first caper tonight, I thought with a mischievous grin as I slowly made my way toward the bread stand. I waited patiently until the baker picked up a tray of bread and carried it into a nearby store. I walked by the stall as casually as I could and snatched a loaf off the cart.

I turned a corner and sat down to eat my stolen prize. Before I could enjoy it, a stray dog approached me. He whined in hunger, his ribs visible against his fur. "You hungry too, pup?" I asked as I ripped off half the loaf for him. He gobbled it down.

I went to take a bite of the remaining bread when a second stray dog walked up to me. He stared at me with a forlorn look in his eyes. With a sad sigh, I gave him the rest of the bread and patted his head. *I guess I won't be eating tonight.*

Then I heard a rumbling sound, and the ground trembled beneath my feet. There was no way my stomach was grumbling *that* loudly!

I quickly followed the source of the sound, weaving through the winding streets of Casablanca. The rumbling got louder and louder until I came upon an ancient stone archway. It was lit from behind with bright lights that made it impossible to see anything beyond it. I stepped toward the blinding white light, shielding my eyes as I went.

As my eyes adjusted, I found myself peering into a giant construction pit. Huge digging machines were clearing dirt from the ground, while workers hunched down on the floor of the pit. They seemed to be using tiny picks and brushes to wipe away soil, though I had no idea why.

"Young lady!" I turned toward the voice. It belonged to a middle-aged man wearing tan khakis and a white shirt. "It's late. Do your parents know where you are?"

I couldn't help but laugh. "Mister, *I* don't even know where I am. What is this place?"

"This is an archaeological dig site," he explained proudly. He waited for me to say something but saw only the confusion in my eyes. "It is where we search for links to our past."

"Like . . . dinosaur bones?" I asked.

"Anything historic." The archaeologist's eyes were shining as he spoke. Clearly he loved nothing more than sharing his passion and knowledge with others. "Even a simple piece of broken pottery can be a magnificent find. Though . . . I am hoping to uncover a little more than that here."

I was trying to pay attention to what he was saying, but my hunger was getting the best of me. I caught a glimpse of a granola bar that was in his pocket and stared at it. My stomach was now grumbling even louder than before.

The archaeologist noticed me staring at his food. "Hungry, are you?" He offered the bar to me with an outstretched hand. I grabbed it and ate it quickly in a few gulps.

"You remind me of my daughter," the archaeologist said, chuckling.

"I do?" I was shocked that I would remind him of anyone. I had never been anyone's daughter before. "What's she like?" I wanted to hear more about his family, but he had already turned back to the dig site.

"If you have been following the news, you'll already know that we just discovered an artifact here. It's very old . . . though not as old as dinosaur bones," he added with a wink.

"What is it?" I asked curiously.

"The Eye of Vishnu! It's one of the most famous jewels in the world, and we've found it!" he exclaimed. "Well . . . the missing one, anyway."

"Missing? Was it stolen?"

"Perhaps it was stolen long ago. That would explain how it traveled here all the way from India, where it was rumored to be from. But mostly it was considered missing because it has never been found until now." Missing artifacts that were thought to be lost to time . . . It was like a real-life adventure!

"See, one Eye of Vishnu is in a museum in Moscow, and it has been there for centuries. It has long been believed that a *second,* matching jewel exists."

I nodded, understanding. "Because everyone has two eyes, right?"

"Exactly!" he cried. "My crew identified the second eye just days ago with our underground imaging technology and is carefully digging it up at this very moment."

I raised an eyebrow. "You're not worried about them stealing it?"

Wouldn't everyone steal a prize such as that? I thought. To my surprise, the archaeologist frowned. He looked disappointed.

"Why would they do that? My crew knows that a treasure such as this belongs in a museum."

"But isn't this treasure worth a fortune?" I asked.

He sighed. "Some things," he said slowly, "possess value that goes beyond how much money they're worth. A historic find such as this gem belongs to everyone. Its theft would rob the world of knowledge and beauty. And that . . . would be a *true crime.*"

"I . . . I never really thought of it that way," I admitted.

My head was spinning. The things the archaeologist was saying were so different from what I had been taught on the island. I had been raised to believe that stealing was like a game—a game without consequences. According to the VILE faculty, crime didn't matter, at least not when it brought money into the organization. To rid the world of knowledge and beauty and history . . . that had to be bad, right?

There was a strange sound, like a computer shutting down, and all around us the floodlights went out. The dig site was plunged into darkness. We were surrounded by an eerie glow as the site was lit only by the light of the full moon.

The archaeologist pulled a walkie-talkie out of his pocket. "Pit crew, report!" He took off toward the dig site.

Suddenly it dawned on me. Gray must have cut the power. *This* was their first caper! The archaeologist had said they were about to dig up a priceless gem—was the Eye of Vishnu their target? It seemed like just the sort of thing the VILE faculty would want to get their hands on. And if Gray was already here, I knew the others were too.

I looked up at the surrounding hills and ruins, my eyes darting back and forth as I tried to spot them in the darkness. Then I saw it—bounding up the security watchtower was the unmistakable silhouette of Le Chèvre. He looked just like a mountain goat as he jumped up the scaffolding toward where the security guards were posted. I watched, my stomach churning, as Le Chèvre knocked down one guard, then another.

There was a loud cry from below. I looked down to see Tigress bounding toward the dig site, her razor-sharp claws shining in the moonlight. With lightning-fast swipes of her hand, she knocked aside workers one by one as she made her way across the excavation.

The ground beneath my feet rumbled once more, but this was not a tremor made by the digging machines. A pile of dirt began to rise up from the bottom of the dig site, and a large hole opened up in the middle of it. Nearby workers scrambled to get away as a figure slowly rose up from the hole in the ground. *El Topo!*

I had seen enough. I raced down toward the dig site, leaping through the construction and into the pit. El Topo brushed dirt off his face. As he saw me, he blinked a few times, finally realizing who was standing in front of him.

"Black Sheep? But I thought you did not graduate."

"Surprise!"

Pale-blue light danced across my eyes. I breathed in sharply at the sight of a gigantic blue gem cradled in his hands.

"It's amazing . . ." I said. And it was. The Eye of Vishnu was the most dazzling thing I had ever seen. None of the jewels I had seen in Countess Cleo's classroom compared to this. It was a massive gem, the size of a football, and its surface was perfectly cut and shaped. Even though it had been buried underground for centuries, there did not appear to be a single scratch on it. It was a beautiful robin's-egg blue that sparkled in the moonlight.

"Black Sheep!" Gray's voice interrupted my trance. "Stay away! You'll ruin the mission!" He was running toward me, fast. There was a fury in his eyes that I had never seen before.

Before I could say anything, I saw the archaeologist

133

coming toward us. He caught sight of the gem in El Topo's hands and stopped in his tracks. He looked from the gem to me, then back again. "You are with *them?*"

"It's complicated." I felt more confused than ever.

The archaeologist started walking toward El Topo. "Stop! Thieves!" he yelled as he pointed to the Eye of Vishnu.

El Topo leaned in toward Gray. "Crackle, remember what they said . . . leave no witnesses."

Gray nodded. I frantically tried to block his path. "Wait, what do you mean, 'leave no witnesses'? Gray?"

El Topo dove back into the tunnel with the Eye of Vishnu in his hands. A shower of dirt rained down over me as he dug underground.

I was gripped by a growing feeling of horror as Gray looked at me with an apologetic expression. He took out the crackle rod that Bellum had made, the one that she had shown us that first day of class all those months ago. He switched it on, then turned the dial up to full power. The crackle rod buzzed and hummed as a dangerous amount of electricity began to charge inside it.

He pointed the rod directly at the archaeologist.

"Gray! No!" I screamed. My heart was pounding fast. I leaped into action.

Gray fired the crackle rod just as I ran into him with everything I had.

The beam of electricity from the rod shot off course, missing the archaeologist by inches. Instead it flew past him and hit the wooden scaffolding lining the ruins, which erupted into flames behind us.

The archaeologist was standing still. He seemed unable to move. He was staring blankly at the smoking spot where the beam had struck, realizing that should've been him.

I didn't know how long it would take for the crackle rod to recharge, and I didn't want to find out. I quickly grabbed the archaeologist by the arm. "Go! Run!"

Realizing his life was in danger, the archaeologist snapped out of his shock and took off at a sprint, fleeing the site as fast as he could.

Gray began to run after the archaeologist, but I stepped in front of him. "Gray, what are you doing? What is wrong with you?" I cried.

"I'll handle the runt!" Tigress's voice came from behind me.

There was no time to think. I lunged forward and grabbed the crackle rod from Gray's hand. I turned the dial down from maximum power and in the same motion spun around to face Sheena.

With a cry of anger that bubbled up from somewhere deep inside me, I pressed the button on the rod, aiming it directly at Tigress. She was blasted with an electric shock that sent her sprawling back into the dirt. I was breathing heavily, stunned by my own feelings of anger and confusion. The shock hadn't been lethal, but she would be unable to move for a few minutes.

I swung the crackle rod toward Gray and approached him angrily. He backed away as much at the sight of the crackle rod as at the furious look on my face.

"What is going on, Gray?" I moved closer to him, the rod crackling with electricity in my hands. "TELL ME!" I raised the rod up to point directly at him.

Suddenly I felt two hands clasp around my mouth. A cloth rag that smelled of strong chemicals was pressed tightly to my face. I struggled wildly, kicking and flailing my arms, but it was no use. I could faintly hear Boris saying that it was time for me to go back to the island as I began to slip out of consciousness.

My vision blurred. I could just barely make out the image of Gray looking at me with a distraught expression on his face. And then everything went dark.

CHAPTER 10

NSIDE THE TRAIN CAR, THE FRENCH COUNTRYSIDE passed by their window, but Carmen was carefully studying Gray.

In his hands was the same crackle rod he had tried to use on the archaeologist, the same one she had stolen for him from Bellum's classroom.

"I thought of you as the big brother I never had, Gray. Until that moment," Carmen said.

Gray looked back at her, his face expressionless. He was not the same Gray that Carmen had met during orientation so long ago. Or at least, she didn't *think* he was. *Maybe I never really knew him at all,* she thought. But maybe . . . just maybe there was a chance that the Gray she used to know was still in there somewhere.

"And you were like a kid sister to me," Gray said quietly after a moment.

"Then what happened?"

"What can I say? Senior seminar was a game-changer . . ."

Gray remembered it all too well. The day after graduation, they had been told to go to a surprise seminar. At the time, he thought it was annoying. Just another class that he would have to take after he thought he was done with them all. Then he found out what the seminar really was . . .

One day after graduating from VILE Academy, Gray stood in the faculty lounge with the other graduates. Next to him were Le Chèvre, El Topo, and Tigress.

Sitting behind the table in their tall chairs, the members of the faculty looked like judges who were about to decide their fates.

Dr. Bellum leaned forward. Gray had always thought her to be a bit scatterbrained, but she gazed at them now with laser-like focus. She cracked her knuckles as she spoke. "Graduates, you did not make it this far on your grades alone. And it is now time for you to face your destiny."

Gray had to keep himself from laughing. Destiny? What were they talking about? He found himself wishing

Black Sheep were here. They would have a good laugh about this later.

It was Maelstrom's turn to speak. "We have been watching you closely all along, to test your loyalty—as well as your ability to go to any . . . *necessary* extremes," he said as he folded his hands slowly in front of him.

Shadowsan stood up. He cast a long, dark shadow over the gathered graduates, and Gray felt a chill run up his spine. The sword, the one hanging in his classroom that Shadowsan had claimed was just for show, was strapped to his waist. Shadowsan took it out of its sheath as he spoke. "No one can stand in the way of achieving our goals . . ."

"For ultimate wealth leads to ultimate power," said Cleo. "You've earned your place in our organization . . ."

Coach Brunt gestured to VILE's logo on the floor in front of them. "Now you will officially join the *Villains' International League of Evil.*"

GRAY LOOKED AT CARMEN ACROSS THE TRAIN CAR AND shrugged. "I guess they knew you didn't have what it takes. They knew you couldn't go to *necessary extremes* to do what needed to be done."

Carmen had listened to his story intently. *So that's*

what I missed in senior seminar, she thought. Much of what Gray told her she had already figured out on her own. From VILE's rule about leaving no witnesses to their belief that wealth was the ultimate form of power . . . But this was the first time she had learned what VILE's initials really stood for.

"Villains' International League of Evil . . ." Carmen repeated slowly. She shook her head. "My entire childhood was a lie. Stealing isn't a game at all. It *does* harm people . . . innocent people!"

Carmen noticed Gray backing away from her against the train seat. She could tell that what she was saying made him uncomfortable.

"Especially when you're willing to steal *lives,*" she added.

"Leave no witnesses," Gray said firmly. "VILE's golden rule."

INSPECTOR CHASE DEVINEAUX WAS BEING TOSSED around the driver's seat of his car like a rag doll as he drove over the rocky terrain alongside the train tracks in pursuit of Carmen Sandiego. He was still chasing her train through the French countryside, and he was determined not to let her slip through his fingers. If she crossed the border, she would no longer be in his territory and he would lose his only chance of catching her.

Though he would never admit it, Chase had been rattled by Carmen Sandiego's actions at the chateau. She had gotten away from him like it was the easiest thing in the world *and* had had fun doing it! *She was toying with me!* Chase was determined to make up for his earlier failing. *It was a fluke, that's all,* he reassured himself. *And it will not happen again.*

Even though his car was bouncing wildly across the hillside, he never took his foot off the gas pedal. He inwardly cursed Interpol for not giving him a car better suited for high-speed train chases.

"Finally!" he yelled as he drove up next to the conductor's window. He quickly took out his badge and waved it back and forth at the window. "Interpol!" he shouted. "Stop this train!"

But the conductor couldn't hear him over the roar of the engine. The train pulled away and the tracks made a sharp turn, leaving the inspector far behind. Chase slammed his hand down on his steering wheel and let out a cry of frustration.

In the seat next to him, his cellphone rang. Chase pressed the speakerphone button angrily. "Inspector Devineaux?" It was Julia.

"What is it now, Ms. Argent? I am driving!" he

responded through his clenched teeth. *This had better be good,* he thought.

"Inspector, I am here at the crime scene. This chateau is filled with stolen goods — money, art . . . Some of it is worth a fortune! There is stolen property here that authorities have been searching for for *years.*"

Chase thought about what Julia was telling him. "I do not understand. Are you saying this was *her* apartment that she was storing stolen goods at? But then why would she steal from herself? It makes no sense!"

"I did some fact-checking," said Julia. "Carmen Sandiego does not own the apartment. In fact, the owner of the chateau is not a person but a company. They seem to specialize in imports and exports. And, even more intriguing," she continued, "the places Carmen Sandiego recently robbed — the Swiss bank, the art gallery in Cairo, the Shanghai amusement park — they all have ties to this same company!"

Chase could feel a headache coming on. "Ms. Argent, what are you trying to say?"

Julia was silent for a moment as she thought about the evidence and began to form a theory in her mind. "What if," she said slowly, "for whatever reason, Carmen Sandiego is a thief . . . who steals only from other thieves?"

"That is ridiculous!" Suddenly, Chase felt his car start

to slow down, even though his foot was still pressing on the gas pedal.

PING!

The car alarm rang loudly. Chase looked down to see a bright letter *E* blinking on and off next to the gas dial.

"Inspector? Is everything all right?" Julia asked, sounding concerned.

"No, everything is not all right, Ms. Argent! My car is out of gas!"

The car came to a sputtering stop by the train tracks. "No, no, no, no, no!" Chase cried, kicking the car in the hopes that he could magically get it to turn on again with the impact.

Chase stepped out of the car with his hands thrust into his pockets. He took out a tin of breath mints and poured all of them into his mouth at once, chewing furiously.

The sound of a roaring engine came from above. Chase looked up to see a small plane passing overhead. It was heading downward, preparing for a landing in the field nearby. *That could get the job done,* he thought with renewed hope.

There wasn't a moment to lose! Chase grabbed his badge and sprinted toward where the plane was about to land.

He came upon it just as its engines were shutting down and the pilots were stepping off the plane. Chase waved his badge high in the air as he shouted, "Interpol! Official business! I am taking over this aircraft!"

CARMEN AND GRAY SAT IN SILENCE ACROSS FROM EACH other in the train car as it chugged steadily along. As always, Carmen was calm and collected. The black satchel containing her stolen prize lay next to her. By now, she knew, Interpol would have found their way into Countess Cleo's chateau, just as she had intended.

Carmen hoped that Player wasn't too worried about her—the EMP that Gray had set off was still in effect, and she had no way of contacting him. She knew that he would be trying to make sure she wasn't in danger. *It's probably a good thing that Player doesn't know I'm with Gray,* she thought.

Gray looked out the window and said, "Our journey's winding to a close." He looked at Carmen with an irritated expression on his face. "And I'm not any closer to knowing the story behind your new look. Or your new name. Carmen Sandiego? Where in the world did *that* come from?"

Carmen smiled. "A lady can't keep a few secrets?"

In response, Gray tapped the crackle rod. Carmen knew all too well what that device was capable of.

"All right. I'll do my best to cut to the chase."

The story behind her name. Now, that was an interesting one . . .

CHAPTER 11

A
FTER THAT NIGHT IN MOROCCO, I AWOKE BACK IN
my room on Vile Island. My Russian nesting dolls
were in their former place on the windowsill next
to my bed, and the map of the world was hanging on the
wall, still without any pins in it. My escape attempt, seeing
the city of Casablanca, my conversation with the archaeologist . . . it all felt like a dream. Like it had never happened.

The memory of what Gray tried to do began to come
back to me, along with Antonio's words. *Leave no witnesses.* I found myself wishing that it *was* all just a bad
dream. Still, I took out a thumbtack and pushed it into
the dot that marked the city of Casablanca in Morocco. I
examined it and sighed. *One place down,* I thought, *and
hundreds more to go.*

Things between the faculty members and me were
different after what happened. I kept expecting to be dis-
ciplined for what I had done, but I received no punishment at all. I suppose they had decided that forcing me to

repeat the school year would be punishment enough. Not to mention I was back on the island, and if I'd felt trapped before, it was like a prison to me now.

But the worst part was that the Cleaners had taken away my phone. They had immediately turned it in to the faculty upon finding it, and I had no way of knowing where it was or what they had done with it. My lifeline to Player, my connection to the outside world, was gone. I was completely alone.

Before the new school year started at VILE Academy, the faculty each dealt with me in their own way. Dr. Bellum thought up new and creative ways to spy on me. Her cameras were hidden, but I became an expert at finding out where they were. I came up with crafty plans to keep away from them as best I could, but I was never really free of her watchful eyes.

Countess Cleo doubled down on her efforts to tame my wild nature and teach me to be a lady. She held what she called "private etiquette lessons." I was, of course, the only student. Cleo would have me walk through the halls each day with a stack of books balanced on my head, sometimes while holding a porcelain cup full of tea. To her credit, my posture never looked better.

Maelstrom would make me take tests that were supposed to tell him things about how my mind worked. I could never figure out what their purpose was. "Japan," I told him one day as he held up a card with a black ink stain on it. To me, the ink stains always looked like different countries of the world. "Wrong!" he said, slamming the card down on the table. "It is a seahorse!"

Shadowsan, on the other hand, avoided me completely, as though I were unworthy of his time or efforts. When we passed each other in the halls, he would always look away as quickly as he could. This was fine by me . . . though sometimes I would jump up and down to try to get his attention, or quickly grab a random small object and ask him if he had dropped it. When he didn't answer, I'd find a way to slip it into his pocket and hope he thought of me when he went to empty his pockets later that night.

And then there was Coach Brunt. Brunt did her best to pretend nothing was wrong and make me feel like a spoiled child again. She was always babying me and bringing me cups of hot chocolate. With tears in her eyes, she would tell me over and over again that she blamed herself for my escape attempt. "We shouldn't have let you enroll in the academy so soon, darlin'. You were too young!" she told me one afternoon.

A year ago, Coach Brunt's coddling would have worked. I would have loved the attention and the warmth of the giant hugs that she gave me as she reassured me that she was still my Mama Bear. But now, after knowing the truth about what VILE did out there in the real world, I no longer wanted to be a part of it.

But even though I wanted nothing to do with VILE, I knew I would have to be careful. If I was going to get through another school year, I would have to be on my very best behavior.

As I tossed and turned in my room each night, I began to come up with a plan. I had no one, not even Player, to talk to this time, but I didn't let that get me down.

Orientation came, and with it the arrival of new students. Just like the year before, Brunt addressed all of us in the auditorium. She talked about the importance of keeping our pasts a secret from one another and of using only our first names. This time, when she said that there would be no cellphones allowed on the island, she was looking straight at me.

I tried to stay calm. I had no idea if the faculty managed to find out about Player, and I couldn't stop worrying that they had. I didn't know what they would do to someone in the outside world who knew about Vile Island's existence. Even though I'd never told Player anything specific about the island, the faculty didn't know I had been so secretive. They would see a hacker who could get through their security as a threat. I sighed. Until I could somehow manage to find the phone—if they hadn't already destroyed it—there was nothing I could do.

Classes started the next day, and I obediently began my year as a VILE student once again. I knew that I'd be way ahead of my new classmates, having already been through the drill. Even so, I decided I would work harder than ever on my coursework. I would be the best student on the island, but all the while, I would be waiting for the right moment to make my move.

I walked into Shadowsan's class full of confidence. If I was going to fool VILE's faculty, I'd have to play the part of someone who still wanted to graduate.

Just as before, Shadowsan told us about the Japanese paper-folding art known as origami and how it would help us become better thieves. He began passing out sheets of folding paper to each student. He stopped when he reached my desk. Shadowsan paused, then dumped a huge stack of origami paper in front of me.

"As you are already familiar with the art of paper folding, Black Sheep, you will fold *all* of these," Shadowsan told me.

I bit my lip angrily but said nothing. *I'll show him,* I thought. If Shadowsan thought I was unruly, I was going to prove him wrong. I knew that he was trying to make me mad by giving me more work to do than anyone else, but I wasn't about to let him succeed.

I picked up the first paper and began to fold it as carefully as I could, quickly crafting a small yet beautiful swan.

I felt someone watching me and turned to see one of my new classmates staring at my work. I recognized her from orientation as a student from Japan, though I didn't know what her skills as a criminal were. Even though she wore the same student uniform as the rest of us, she had found ways to work all sorts of bright colors into her hair and her fashionable accessories.

I quickly completed my swan. The girl was looking at me the entire time I folded.

She was starting to make me nervous, so I decided to try talking to her. "Pretty boring stuff, huh? Too bad we don't get to use swords and things, like real ninjas."

She quickly turned back to her own origami, which I saw she was folding into a paper lily. "Actually, I like this . . . *stuff*," she answered with a toss of her hair. "Could I have some of your folding paper? Instructor Shadowsan gave me only one."

"Sure, knock yourself out," I said as I gave her a giant stack.

As the days went on, I studied as hard as I possibly could. Anyone who observed me at the academy would think I was more determined than ever.

Coach Brunt was pleased to see me fighting up a storm in her self-defense class, which I now knew was actually meant to teach us how to "leave no witnesses" out in the field. I picked more pockets in Shadowsan's class and pointed out more fake paintings in Countess Cleo's than anyone else. I was even at the top of my game in Dr. Bellum's science class, which had never been my best subject.

Slowly but surely, my plan was working. The faculty members stopped spying on me as much, and Maelstrom stopped giving me his silly tests. I still caught Bellum's flying cameras following me around the island, but the more I acted like I wanted to be the best VILE operative in history, the more freedom I was granted.

One afternoon, Cleo was having me sit through a pretend dinner party and she actually told me that I was becoming more ladylike by the day. I smiled and politely thanked her. It was taking all my focus to keep up the charade, but my training was helping.

I avoided my classmates, being careful not to form any new friendships. I ate meals alone and walked to and from classes by myself. Some, like the girl from Shadowsan's class, tried to speak to me now and then, but I did my best to ignore them. I soon developed a reputation for being snooty—a know-it-all who thought she was better than everyone else. I didn't let it get to me.

I had no doubt that my classmates would go to the "necessary extremes" after they graduated, just like Gray and the others. My old classmates had been skilled criminals, but these new students were tough and fierce in a way that surprised even me.

We sat on the mats one day in Shadowsan's class. We were, as usual, folding origami figures. This time Shadowsan had given me a *hundred* pieces of paper to fold. Everyone else had just ten. I went about my work silently, determined not to give Shadowsan a reason to think I was still a troublemaker.

"Can I have some of your paper?" asked the Japanese girl again.

Once again, I slid her a stack of paper with a shrug.

The folding came as easily to me as ever, and before long, I had a set of origami animals sitting across my desk.

"That's pretty good," she said, examining my work.

"Thanks." I wondered for a moment if she was looking to get help with her own paper folding. Most of the students were struggling with the task. When I looked over to her desk to see how her origami was coming along, my jaw dropped.

She had folded an entire army of Japanese soldiers. The folds were perfect—more perfect than anything I had ever been able to do. She had even given them miniature paper swords and bows with tiny quivers of arrows.

I had never seen anything like it. "That's . . . that's amazing," I told her, and meant it.

The girl laughed. Her laugh sounded like nails dragging across a chalkboard, and I immediately got chills. "What, these? These were just for fun! Look what else I can do!" She took out a single sheet of origami paper and quickly began folding it.

Her fingers were moving too fast for me to follow. In no time at all, the girl had turned the paper into a star. Only it didn't seem to be just any star — it was more like a ninja's throwing star, with dangerously sharp edges.

With a flick of her wrist, she threw the paper star toward the origami soldiers. At first, nothing happened. And then, one by one, each of the soldiers fell apart. They had been cut perfectly in half by the sharp slice of the star.

"See? Pretty cool, huh?" she said.

I stared at her and laughed nervously. "That's, uh . . . something, all right." I didn't want to let on that she made me wildly uncomfortable. For someone to pick up skills like that within the first few weeks of classes . . . well, it was impressive, but also a little scary.

"Call me Paperstar. It's my code name," she told me with a wicked smile. "You're the only one who knows it."

"Paperstar, huh? That's a good one." I made a mental note to stay as far away from her as possible.

CHAPTER 12

A FTER WEEKS OF PREPARATION AND PLANNING, the day I had been waiting for finally came. It was December first—the day Cookie Booker's boat arrived on the island.

Early that morning, I had told Coach Brunt that I was feeling ill and would not be able to attend classes that day. She had chicken noodle soup sent to my room, along with hot tea. For a moment, I was touched. Mama Bear still cared about me. But I knew I couldn't let this one small gesture change anything.

The weather outside was gloomy and ominous. Storm clouds gathered overhead, and in the distance, there was a bright orange flash as lightning struck over the ocean. Rain began to come down, at first in a small drizzle and then in a heavy downpour. It was almost time.

I ran from my room, through the hallways and out into the storm. I wasn't able to see the docks from the dormitory, so in order to make sure the boat was arriving as scheduled,

I made my way down to the beach. *I have to be sure it's here,* I thought. *Everything has to go according to plan.*

I had no water balloons with me this time as I watched and waited by the rocks. My pranking days were over; this time, I was playing for real. And then I saw it—the boat! In the distance, I could see it sailing across choppy waters toward the docks. I had seen it at least a dozen times or more over the years, but never with the kind of anticipation I felt now.

Cookie Booker was right on time. *Boy, she must really hate this weather,* I thought, and I laughed at how someone who hated water as much as she did was now stuck on a boat in a storm.

Once I knew that the boat was arriving, I dashed back to my room to grab what few possessions I had.

At the academy, we had been taught over and over again to travel light. I could hear Maelstrom's voice in my mind. "Carry too much with you, and it could slow you down. If you are slowed down, you cannot do your job properly. Always, *always,* travel light!" Maelstrom might be a crazy professor, but I knew he was right.

I carefully picked up my Russian nesting dolls. They were the only link I had to my past. I touched a hand to the dolls, tracing their red edges as I had a million times before. *Travel light,* I thought, and sadly set them back down.

Instead I grabbed my stealth suit. In the past, I used

to daydream about wearing it while stealing for VILE. Now I would be using it to escape from them. I quickly changed into it, feeling readier by the moment. I snuck out of the room, leaving the nesting dolls behind.

Shadowsan's stealth training was being put to good use as I silently hurried through the academy. I was almost to the front doors when the sound of Maelstrom's voice suddenly made me stop.

"I find it strange that a device registered to our mainland Bookkeeping Department ever wound up in Black Sheep's possession to begin with," he said.

"And *I* find it strange that Black Sheep never submitted the stolen property for extra credit," I heard Dr. Bellum reply.

I edged closer to the door, careful to remain unseen. I could see Professor Maelstrom and Dr. Bellum inside a study room. Maelstrom was pacing the room, looking closely at something in front of him. I peered carefully around the doorframe and gasped as I saw my cellphone on the desk in front of them.

Player! I almost said his name out loud in excitement. Was he all right? Had they tried to contact him? It had been months since I had talked to him, and I suddenly felt desperate to hear my friend's voice again.

Bellum took the phone and placed it in a desk drawer, then locked it and put the key in her pocket.

"Perhaps Ms. Booker can fill us in on the details," Maelstrom said. Bellum and Maelstrom left, and I quickly hid behind the office door. I held my breath, not daring to breathe again until I was sure they were out of sight.

Once the coast was clear, I hurried inside and raced to the desk. I took out a bobby pin and inserted it into the lock. After a few tries, the lock snapped open. *For a school that teaches criminals,* I thought, *you would think their locks would be harder to pick.*

The drawer slid open, and there it was — my phone! I grabbed it and hid out of sight beneath the desk. Then I hit autodial.

"Becky's Bacon and Barbecue House. Can I help you?" Player was speaking in a high-pitched voice with a thick southern accent, but it was still unmistakably Player.

"Player? That you?" I asked.

"Black Sheep! You bet it's me. I was just being careful."

I breathed a sigh of relief. Words couldn't describe how good it felt to hear the voice of my only real friend after months of isolation.

"Where have you been?" Player asked. "Strange people have been answering your phone!"

"It's not my phone," I admitted. "I stole it."

Player was silent for a moment as he thought about what I had just said. "So you're a shoplifter . . . and you haven't called me all summer because you've been in jail?"

I sighed. I had kept everything about Vile Island hidden from Player for years. But now I was done keeping VILE's secrets for them.

"Player, remember when you told me you use your awesome hacking skills for good?"

"The white-hat hacker's code," he said with pride.

"What would you say if I had awesome skills too . . . because I was raised in a school for thieves?"

There was silence on the other end of the line. I nervously bit my lip. Had I just scared off my only friend in the world?

"I would say that explains a lot!" Player almost sounded excited.

Our conversation was interrupted by the sound of approaching footsteps. "Don't go anywhere," I whispered to Player. The footsteps were coming straight toward me.

There was no time to escape from the room without being seen, and there were no windows, either. Instead, the answer to my problems came from above.

From where I was crouched, I could see an air vent. The screws looked loose and easy to remove. My stealth suit was already coming in handy as I jumped from the desk toward the vent, leaping through the air like an Olympic gymnast. I grasped the vent and pulled it away from its frame, then climbed up into the ceiling. I quickly put the vent back into its frame just as the shadow of a figure crossed into the room.

I moved through the ceiling, crawling through the narrow passages as quickly as the tight space would allow. As I moved past another vent, what I saw below me made me stop immediately.

Sitting on the desk below was the VILE hard drive —the one that Cookie Booker delivered by hand to the island each year on this day. The VILE logo was emblazoned on its side.

"Player, I'm staring at a hard drive containing data that could fund a criminal organization for an entire year," I told him in a whisper. It was strange to think that something so small had such important information stored within it. Right then, I knew what I had to do. "This might be my only chance to secure it," I told him.

"Then you have to go for it."

I smiled, glad to have someone on my side when I was about to try to pull off the most dangerous theft of my life. Stealing the hard drive hadn't been part of my escape plan, but I realized now that it had to be done. They would use the hard drive to plan their future criminal operations. If I took it from them, maybe I could keep them from hurting innocent people.

I dropped into the room as quietly as a ninja. The

hard drive was just a few feet away. I reached out for it, my fingers almost touching it, when suddenly I heard Maelstrom's booming voice come from the intercom sitting on the desk. "Booker, what is keeping you? We are waiting for you to upload the hard drive!" I jumped at the sound.

Then I heard stiletto shoes clicking on tiles and ducked beneath the desk, tucking my knees up toward my chest.

From a crack in the desk, I was able to see Cookie Booker walk into the room. She was wearing a stylish black pantsuit and a yellow scarf slung over her shoulders. She was also soaking wet and quite angry about it.

Booker pressed the intercom with her hand. "Have you never heard of a thunderstorm, Gunnar Maelstrom? I had to hang my wet things!" She grabbed the hard drive from the desk and stomped off.

I slammed a hand against the back of the desk. "I missed it! The hard drive is gone!"

"What are you going to do?" asked Player.

"I'm going after it," I said. I crept out from under the desk, full of determination. The boat would have to wait.

CHAPTER 13

FOLLOWED COOKIE BOOKER AT A SAFE DISTANCE AS she made her way through the academy halls. I had to work to keep my nerves in check as I carefully tracked her, making sure not to get too close.

"If anyone sees me take it, I'll never make it off the island," I whispered into the phone.

"You mean the island I still can't locate?"

"That's the one. I need to avoid getting caught at all costs. Otherwise . . . it's game over."

I was walking past a darkened corridor when suddenly I felt like I was being watched. It was just like that night on the rocks when I escaped from the island. Once again, I saw a pale face in the darkness watching me, only this time I didn't pass it off as my imagination.

I stopped and walked closer. Mime Bomb was there, leaning against the wall as though he didn't have a care in the world. "Aw, crud," I whispered under my breath.

"Mime Bomb!" I said with a huge smile, hiding the cellphone behind my back. "What are you up to?"

Mime Bomb waved hello and pretended to pick invisible flowers. He held the imaginary flowers up to his nose and sniffed them.

I made a guess. "Stopping to smell the roses?"

He nodded to tell me I was correct.

"Happy gardening!" I turned and started walking off again, hoping I hadn't lost track of Cookie Booker and the hard drive.

"That was the most one-sided conversation I've ever heard," Player said, confused.

"Don't worry. It's just some creepy mime who hangs around campus and watches everything . . . and everyone . . ." Suddenly I realized what Mime Bomb really was. "Because he's a snitch and a spy for the faculty!"

Eyes and ears . . . just like he said during Cleo's exam! I smacked my forehead. How had I been so stupid? It was Mime Bomb who told the faculty I snuck onto the helicopter. That was how the Cleaners knew I had stowed away! I was not going to let him tell on me a second time.

I turned back to where Mime Bomb had been just a moment before, but he was already gone. I sprinted down the corridor, catching up to him in no time. He looked behind him with an alarmed expression.

"Nobody likes a tattletale!" I yelled as I made a running

slide across the tile. I slid right into Mime Bomb's legs, knocking him off his feet.

Getting him into the supply closet wasn't easy, but I managed to shove him in, making sure to grab the handyman's toolkit from the shelf before he could use it to pick the lock. With Mime Bomb locked inside and the toolkit in hand, I set off after Cookie Booker again.

I sprinted through the halls, almost running out of breath. "I hope I didn't lose her, Player," I said as I frantically went from one corridor to another. Finally, I caught sight of a yellow scarf. I skidded to a halt, ducking for cover behind a post.

Cookie Booker was standing in front of an elevator at the end of a hallway. I watched as she took out a keycard and swiped it on the elevator control pad. The light on the pad turned green. My eyes widened. "You need a keycard to use that elevator. If she makes it to the server room and I'm not there to stop her, she'll upload the data from the hard drive!"

"So let me get this straight," Player said. "You can't let anyone see you take the hard drive, but if she uploads it before you can get it, then VILE will get all the information that's stored on it and—"

"And they win. I better think fast!" I ran toward the elevator. Cookie had stepped inside with the hard drive in hand, and the doors were closing. I went for it at the last second, sliding into the elevator like a baseball player sliding into home base.

"What on earth—" Cookie Booker said, startled by my sudden entrance. I jumped up quickly and gave her a smile and a wave. She simply stared at me, taking in my messy appearance with a frown. I knew I had to think of a lie quickly if I didn't want her to sound the alarm.

"Sorry if I scared you, ma'am," I said in my most adult-sounding voice. "I work for VILE's tech department, and I've been ordered to check the server room pronto for, uh, loose cables!" I tapped on the toolkit that I was still carrying in my hands.

I could feel Booker's eyes on me as she looked me up and down. The seconds ticked by, and still she said nothing. "I guess we both got the 'Wear black' memo today," I offered. I glanced up at her to see her reaction, and to my horror, I saw her upper lip curl into a sneer.

"My, my, how you've grown," she said.

I gulped and took a deep breath. "Yes, I have grown. And with age comes maturity . . . which is why I was trying to find you, Ms. Booker. So we could talk." I gestured around to the elevator. "Somewhere private! I just wanted you to know how ashamed I am of the dumb pranks I pulled on you over the years. I apologize." I said all this as sincerely as I could, and I held my breath as she thought about what I said.

Finally, after what felt like ages, she spoke. "I wondered why there was no water balloon attack tonight—first time without one in quite a few years."

All I could think to do was shrug guiltily. "Yeah . . . sorry about that. I know you hate water."

"Oh? I suppose word gets around, doesn't it?" Her expression changed into a more caring smile. "I'll blame your actions on your unusual upbringing. One can't be expected to behave honorably when raised among thieves, after all."

I gave her the sweetest smile I knew how to give and extended my hand. "Shake on it, Ms. Booker?" She shook my hand, and I breathed a sigh of relief.

"Please, call me Cookie."

The elevator doors opened. We had arrived at the server room. Cookie stepped out and turned back to me. "Young lady, you seem like a smart cookie. Take my advice—set your sights higher than pulling pranks or picking pockets. Try stealing from businesses, like I do. That's where the real money is. You can count on it."

"Thank you. I'll take that to heart."

Cookie Booker waved her hand over her head like a pageant queen. "*Arrivederci!*" She headed for the servers.

The doors closed, and the elevator began its ride back up. "A successful bait and switch if I do say so myself," I told Player with a mischievous grin.

"What's a bait and switch?" he asked.

"It's when you switch the object you're stealing with something else without anyone knowing," I explained. "Like what I just did with the hard drive."

I held up the VILE hard drive, which was now in my hands. Any moment now, Cookie Booker would realize that I had switched the drive for the toolkit I had taken from the closet. *Maelstrom would be proud,* I thought.

"Nice going, Black Sheep!"

"That wasn't even the hard part. Now I need to get out of here."

The elevator doors opened into the academy corridor. I slowly stepped out into the hallway, keeping the hard drive close at my side.

Suddenly, the lights went off. The entire building was plunged into darkness—though the darkness didn't last long. Seconds later, crimson lights cast an eerie red glow through the halls.

"*Code red.* They're onto me." Code red meant that someone had sounded the alarm and the entire island was going into lockdown. There was no response on the other end of the line. "Player? Hello?" No answer. They had jammed the cellular signals. I was completely on my own now.

Of course I had known that Cookie would notice the switch when she went to upload the drive to the servers, but I hoped I would have a few more minutes before she sounded the alarm so I could get a head start. The plan had been to make it outside before anyone realized what I had done. Now I would have to make my escape while everyone on the island was looking for me.

I suddenly realized how much danger I was in. I no longer cared if anyone saw me. The only thing that mattered was getting out. *The storm drain!* It worked during my last escape attempt, and I hoped it would again.

I raced through the halls until I made it to my destination. I was out of breath, but adrenaline flowed through my veins. I leaped into the storm drain and crawled along it as fast as I could, fighting against the rushing water.

Finally I made it to the grate that led to the outside, and I pushed on it. It didn't budge. I pushed again as hard as I could, feeling the panic set in. Then I saw with horror that it had been screwed shut from the other side. The faculty had figured out how I escaped last time . . . and they made sure I would not be able to do it again.

I sat against the grate, hugging my knees. I felt exhausted, and for the first time I wondered if there was any way I was going to make it off the island. All my planning had led to nothing. I had ruined my chance at escaping for good — and there was no way the faculty were going to let me off easy this time.

I tried to fight back the tears that were stinging my

eyes. I looked at the hard drive. The data that was on that drive would keep VILE going for another year. With it, they could do horrible things, like what they had done in Casablanca.

I thought about what the archaeologist had told me. Some things had value that went beyond how much money they were worth. VILE had never understood that, and they never would. *Someone has to stop them,* I thought.

I stood up and wiped my tears away with the back of my hand, feeling my courage returning. *I'm going to get off this island,* I thought with a sudden a rush of confidence as I started heading back the way I had come.

I made it back to the academy building, staying close to the corners and the walls as I went. The red lights were still glowing everywhere. I was making my way past the faculty lounge when I heard a familiar voice and stopped.

"It's past curfew. All students are accounted for, except . . ." Coach Brunt sounded sad.

"Black Sheep," said Shadowsan. There was something about the way he said my name that made me deeply afraid.

"Enough is enough. The child must be punished," said Cleo.

I leaned closer to the door to watch their meeting. Cleo nodded to Shadowsan. He put a hand to the sword that hung at his side, and I felt my heart stop for a beat.

If I didn't make it off the island right now, that would be it for me!

I turned to leave, but before I could make my escape, I heard a familiar set of high-heeled shoes coming toward me. I hid behind the door as Cookie Booker walked into the faculty room.

"Maelstrom, the child is a nuisance, but placing the entire island on lockdown? Is that really necessary?" Cookie stomped her foot. "I wish to go immediately!"

"The 'child' has stolen precious VILE data, and it was all thanks to you! We must retrieve that hard drive at any cost!" Maelstrom fired back as I clutched the drive closer to my chest.

"Well, it's out of my hands now. Please give me permission to leave!" Cookie's hands were on her hips, and she was looking from one faculty member to another.

Maelstrom waved his hand impatiently in Cookie's direction. "Fine! Good riddance. Hurry back to the mainland, where it is dry."

I gasped. If Cookie had been given permission to leave the island, that meant the boat would be leaving too, and soon.

"Very well. I'll collect my coat and be off."

Suddenly, I had an idea. But if it was going to work, I would have to act fast.

I took off down the corridor. I was not about to wait

around and give Shadowsan an opportunity to use his sword.

I hurried to the study room where Cookie Booker had stored her things upon arrival. I opened the closets and searched through them until I found what I was looking for — Cookie Booker's hat and raincoat.

"Code red . . ." I whispered to myself as I looked at the crimson-red hat and trench coat hanging in front of me. There was no time to lose. I grabbed them both.

The sound of Cookie's heels on the tiles was getting closer and closer. I hid behind the door and watched silently as she came into the room. When she walked over to the closet and saw that her coat and hat were missing, she gave an angry cry of frustration. "I hate this island!" she yelled.

I smiled and carefully waited until she came close enough to reach.

CHAPTER 14

AHEAD OF ME, I COULD SEE VLAD AND BORIS standing guard by the main entrance. I had to get past them if I wanted to make it out to the docks. Their walkie-talkies crackled with the sound of Maelstrom's voice. "Cleaners, our bookkeeper has caused enough damage for one visit. Allow her to leave, or get rid of her. I won't stop you either way!"

Here goes, I thought. It was time to see if this disguise would actually work. I adjusted the red hat on my head, keeping it tilted down so that the Cleaners wouldn't be able to see my face.

I started to walk toward them briskly, my heels click-clacking loudly on the lobby floor as I approached them. The stilts I had just stolen from Coach Brunt's gymnasium were working like a charm. They rested in the heels of my shoes, making me the same height as Cookie Booker. Fortunately, I'd had plenty of practice using them. I reached Vlad and Boris. My heart was pounding so fast that I was sure it would jump out of my chest. Coach Brunt used to tell me that nothing ever slipped past the watchful eyes of the Cleaners, but I had no choice now. I had to risk it.

"Ms. Booker?" Vlad asked.

I stayed silent, holding my breath. I was certain that the ruse was up. *This is it,* I thought. *It's over.*

"Until next year, Ms. Booker," Vlad said, sounding sincerely sorry to see me go.

"Bon voyage," Boris added, and nodded a goodbye.

I nodded back, dipping my fedora even lower. As I continued past them, I gave a pageant wave, twirling my hand exactly as I had seen Cookie Booker do just a short while before. *"Arrivederci,"* I said in my shrillest imitation of Cookie's voice.

I pushed through the doors and stepped out into the storm. Wind whipped at my face, and the cold rain soaked through my clothes. I expected to hear shouts from behind me at any moment, but they never came.

I quickened my pace. The stilts were slipping on the wet rocks, and I struggled to walk in Cookie's high-heeled shoes. They wobbled dangerously on the stone steps as I made my way down.

Any moment now, they would find Cookie Booker bound and gagged in the closet where I had left her. I did feel a *little* guilty about that — she had been sort of nice to me, in her own way. But my life depended on getting off this island tonight.

I finally made it to the docks. I breathed a sigh of relief when I saw that the boat was still waiting. Tall waves were crashing against the boat's side as it rocked back and forth in the storm.

My bright red attire was a spot of color amid the dark skies. It was such a bold choice of color, in fact, that wearing it somehow made me feel more courageous.

I was almost at the boat now. I could see the boat's captain, the same man I had stolen the cellphone from, looking at me from where he stood on the deck. I could faintly hear his walkie-talkie turn on and the sound of Maelstrom's voice coming through it. "Captain, be on alert. The lady in red is no lady at all, but a girl . . . with a history of throwing water balloons." This was the captain's chance for payback, and I knew he wouldn't want to squander it.

I quickly pulled the hat down farther to cover my face as the captain tried to make out my identity. After hearing nothing from the boat, I carefully looked up. I gasped.

He was holding a harpoon, the kind that could fire a spear directly at me. The captain hoisted it up to point it toward me, readying it for firing.

There was no time to think. I ran across the dock and leaped into the air, jumping high above the boat. My coat fluttered behind me while I focused on my target. As I came down toward the deck of the boat, I grabbed one of the stilts from beneath my feet, pulled back my arm, and threw it at the captain.

The stilt whirled through the air like a boomerang.

SMACK!

It hit its target with a perfect bull's-eye. The captain fell backwards and tumbled off the deck. There was a small thud as he landed on the sandy shores. He moaned, holding his head in his hands. He had landed on the harpoon, snapping it in half.

A figure on the rocks was running quickly in the direction of the boat. *Too* quickly. I saw a bright flash of light and with dawning terror recognized it as a glint of steel reflecting the moonlight. It was Shadowsan, with his unsheathed samurai sword in hand.

I raced to the boat controls. I began pressing buttons, but . . . nothing happened. The engine refused to turn on. I slammed my fist on the control panels. "Come *on!*" I yelled as panic began to set in. Suddenly, I remembered that the captain had a set of keys around his belt. They must be needed to start the engine.

Shadowsan was still running straight toward me and getting close. I jumped from the boat onto the shore where the captain lay unconscious. I grabbed for the keys, struggling to get them free. With every passing second,

I could feel Shadowsan getting closer. I forced myself to stay calm. Finally the keys came away.

I ran back to the boat and slammed the key into the ignition. The engine sputtered and then came to life. *Now, that's more like it,* I thought.

"Black Sheep!" Shadowsan roared, his voice becoming one with the storm.

The boat still didn't move. "Oh, *no* . . ." I said aloud. I slapped and kicked at the controls desperately.

From the corner of my eye, I could see that Shadowsan was at the docks now.

My hands shaking, I saw a lever next to the steering wheel and pushed it forward. I was thrown back as the boat suddenly moved, sending a shower of water splashing against the dock at Shadowsan's feet.

Shadowsan watched the boat pull away from the island —with me, a red-coated figure standing tall on its deck.

He and I looked at each other, only this time, I was unafraid. I picked up the red hat from where it had fallen on the deck of the boat and placed it back on my head.

Shadowsan became smaller and smaller in the distance. I saw him sheath his sword, and I exhaled with relief. I hadn't even realized that I had been holding my breath for so long. "I pass. You fail," I whispered.

I grabbed the wheel to steady the boat's course. I looked back only once. The academy buildings had disappeared, and the island was nothing more than a speck of sand and palm trees in the distance. *I had done it!* I was finally leaving Vile Island. I did not know if I would ever again see the place I had called home for so many years. *I hope not,* I thought as lightning lit up the sky. Then darkness returned, and the island disappeared from view entirely.

I picked up the hard drive and examined it closely as a plan began to form in my mind.

CHAPTER 15

THE TRAIN'S BRAKES SQUEALED, SNAPPING CARMEN back to the present. "It's the end of the line," Gray said as the train neared the station—the last stop on its journey. Carmen nodded.

Gray leaned forward, crackle rod still in hand. The time had come for him to give Carmen the message he had been sent to deliver. "VILE misses you, Black Sheep. They want a truce."

"Misses me?" Carmen asked angrily. "They just want me stealing *for* them instead of *from* them. All VILE wants is to control me."

"You've proven yourself to them. To *us*. Isn't that all you ever wanted?"

Carmen said nothing. She sensed there was something Gray wasn't telling her.

"The faculty are offering you a full pardon. Even Shadowsan's on board!" Gray continued. "They'll make things right if you just come home to the island . . . where you belong."

Carmen sighed. Whether or not she was considering Gray's offer was unclear to him.

"I *was* hoping we would end up on the same side tonight, Gray," Carmen said. She paused and looked at him with a steady gaze. "*My* side."

"Still in a league of your own," he said.

"Always was, always will be."

Gray nodded slowly, then raised the crackle rod. It began to buzz and hum with electricity as he cranked the dial all the way up to its full, deadly level of power.

Carmen was not afraid. Instead, she raised an eyebrow at Gray. "Does this mean you don't want to know how I got my new code name?"

Gray hadn't been expecting a question like that. He hesitated a moment.

That was all the time a trained thief like Carmen needed. She lunged for the rod, catching Gray off-guard, and grabbed it from him so quickly that he barely saw her move. In a split second, Carmen was pointing the crackle rod at Gray.

"I added a fingerprint sensor. It'll work only for me," Gray told her triumphantly.

Carmen shrugged. "Then it's a tie."

Suddenly, the windows began to shake and Gray

covered his ears as the deafening sound of an engine came from outside the train car.

Right outside the window was a small plane flying alongside the moving train. In the pilot seat was a furious Frenchman who seemed to be shouting something at them while waving a badge around. "What the blazes . . . ?" Gray said, distracted by the sight of the madman in the plane.

Gray remembered that Carmen still held the crackle rod and turned back to her. But he was a moment too late. Carmen swung it over her head.

WHACK!

Gray fell forward, his face pressing against the window. With a loud squeak, he slowly slid to the floor. Carmen snapped the crackle rod in two as he went down.

"Red! You're back online!" Player said through her earpiece.

"Glad to have you back with me, Player."

"Did I miss anything?"

Carmen stepped toward Gray, who was lying unconscious on the floor. "Nothing you didn't already know. But I had to fill in a few details for Gray." The memories swept over her . . .

CHAPTER 16

I REMEMBER THAT VOYAGE ACROSS THE SEA LIKE IT WAS yesterday. The boat moved up and down over the stormy waves while I steered it carefully along.

I felt a buzz in my pocket. I took out my phone to see the white hat and immediately answered. "Player!" I cried, happy to have him back with me. "I made it! I'm off the island," I told him.

"You did it! I knew you could!"

"I need your help. I need to know where I am!" It was no good trying to direct the boat if I had no idea where in the world I was.

"Tracing your position . . . You're near the Canary Islands, a Spanish settlement just off the coast of—"

"West Africa!" I had another pin to put in the world map, it seemed. "Now it's time to see the rest of the world. Are you with me, Player? I could use some tech support."

"You know it!" I could almost hear him pumping the air with his fist through the phone. "When do we start?"

I thought his question over as I gripped the wheel of the boat tightly, the rain splashing against my face. "Right now."

The wind flapped against the brim of my hat, causing it to hit my face over and over again. Annoyed, I took it off, preparing to toss it out into the ocean like a frisbee. "No more VILE," I said firmly.

"You'll need a passport if you want to travel, which means you'll have to use a different name. Black Sheep isn't going to cut it. You do have a real name, don't you?" Player didn't know that Black Sheep was never just a code name for me. It was the only name I had ever had.

Something on the hat caught my eye. It was the label, sewn into the side of it. I brought it closer to read it. "Carmen Brand Outerwear . . ." I read. It was printed in a large, curly font. Then, in smaller words below, it said, "Made in San Diego, California."

The wind whipped my hair. I pulled the red trench coat tighter around me, feeling my confidence growing by the second.

"My name is Carmen. Carmen Sandiego," I told him with a smile. It had a nice ring to it. "Now . . . about this white-hat hacker thing," I said as I flipped the bright red hat back onto my head and pulled it down across my face. "Does it have to be white?"

CHAPTER 17

NSPECTOR CHASE DEVINEAUX COULD SEE THE THIEF'S
red fedora from where he stood in the train's narrow
hallway. "Carmen Sandiego . . . I've got you now," he
growled under his breath as he raced toward her train car.
He caught a glimpse of her trench coat from behind the
glass window. *There is nowhere for her to hide, nowhere for
her to escape to!* Chase thought happily as he reached the
door to her car.

He burst into the compartment, his badge in his hand.
"Carmen Sandiego, you are under arrest!"

Chase saw what looked to be Carmen Sandiego herself, slumped over in the train seat. Her hat was covering
her face. It looked as though she was sleeping. *Is the super
thief taking a nap? Has she foolishly let her guard down?* he
wondered.

This was not how he had imagined the arrest of the
great Carmen Sandiego happening. He had been hoping
for a more exciting capture that would be spoken of by

everyone at Interpol for years to come. Nevertheless, he had still captured her.

Chase lifted the hat from her face and jumped backwards. Slumped unconscious on the train seat was not a woman, but a young man. His ankles and wrists were tied. "What?" the inspector cried aloud. Who was this man, and where was . . . ? *Oh no,* he thought.

Chase ran to the window and looked toward the train platform. Suddenly, his eyes were drawn to a flash of red in the crowd. His eyes went wide. For the briefest of moments, he could see the shape of Carmen Sandiego in her bright red trench coat. *It's her!* She was making her way through the crowds on the platform.

The train slowly began to pull away from the station. A pillar crossed in front of Chase's vision, just for a moment. When he looked at the station again, she was gone.

Chase slammed his fist on the window angrily. "No! Not again!"

He felt his cellphone ring, and he answered it.

"Yes?"

"Inspector Devineaux," said Julia Argent, "we've turned up something rather amazing."

"Well? What is it?" Chase asked as he rubbed his forehead.

"We believe it's the second Eye of Vishnu. The one

from the unsolved Morocco heist? We found it right there in the chateau, almost as if—"

"Let me guess... almost as if Carmen Sandiego wanted us to find it!" Chase could feel a headache coming on, and what he was hearing was only making it worse. He popped some more mints into his mouth.

"Why else would she have left behind such a rare and valuable artifact, Inspector? When that heist in Morocco happened and the Eye of Vishnu was stolen, it was a terrible loss to the historical community. Perhaps she wanted it put back in the right hands. To make sure it would go to a museum."

Chase shook his head. *No,* he thought. *A thief is a thief.*

"If she left the Eye of Vishnu behind," Chase said, "then what was in her black satchel? She must have gotten away with something else—something truly priceless!"

A MOTORBOAT CRUISED DOWN THE CALM WATERS OF THE Seine river in France. Unlike Carmen Sandiego's daring escape from Vile Island, this boat trip was peaceful and relaxing.

"I can't believe you didn't take the gemstone!" Player said in disbelief. He had just found out about Carmen's little bait and switch. "That thing was the size of my head!"

"It was a total win-win," Carmen said with a smile. "I knew Interpol would get it back where it belonged, which left my hands free to take the real treasure."

"The real treasure?"

Carmen opened the black bag and carefully took out the object that was inside. She held the Russian nesting dolls tightly in her hands, her fingers once again tracing the familiar swirls of red paint. It felt like a lifetime ago that she had left them behind on the night of her escape. She hadn't realized then just how much she would miss them.

"My oldest companions. They're like an archaeological find . . . the only link I have to my past." She turned them over. On the bottom of the largest doll was a metal sticker that was blinking red. It was the tracker that VILE had used to trace her location.

"VILE knew I would take these dolls. They were using them to get to me."

Carmen peeled off the tracker. There was a boat approaching her from the opposite direction. *Let's send them on a wild goose chase,* she thought, and slapped the tracker on the side of the passing boat.

"Now, did you send the money from the Shanghai job to the charities on my list?"

"Food bank, homeless shelter, orphanage—check!"

Carmen smiled. She and Player kept whatever money they needed for their operations, but the rest always went to the people who needed it most.

"I even had time to decode the next entry from the VILE hard drive," Player said. "It's another secret hide-out."

"Where to this time?"

"It's located in Southeast Asia, on the island of Java in Indonesia."

Carmen chuckled. "Just when I thought I was through with islands."

Sparkling light began to dance across the water, and Carmen looked up to see the Eiffel Tower spectacularly lit up against the darkening night sky. Parisians and tourists alike were walking the city streets hand in hand and sitting at the small sidewalk cafés.

Carmen pulled her coat tighter. "Paris isn't going anywhere. We need to stay one step ahead of VILE while we have the advantage."

"I'll book you a flight."

The boat sped off down the river, passing through Paris and all its spectacular nighttime beauty.

After her escape from the island, the first thing Carmen had done was mail the stolen VILE hard drive to Player. Her instincts had been right—the layers of security encryptions that protected the files on it were no match for Player's awesome hacking skills.

The second thing she had done was travel. She had wanted to see the world, and that's exactly what she had set out to do. Carmen traveled every chance she got, trying new things, seeing incredible landmarks, and experiencing as much history and culture as she could. It hadn't all been play, of course . . . she had also been training hard and making her plans to take down VILE. With the hard drive in their possession, Player was able to locate VILE's operations and heists. The rest was up to the great Carmen Sandiego.

Carmen adjusted her red fedora. She knew her mission in life would continue to allow her to see the far corners of the world, and she had never been to Indonesia before. She was excited by this sudden realization and steered the boat toward the airport. Another new place to see—who knew what kind of excitement would be in store for her there?

"We're off to Indonesia," she said.

And with a bright streak of red against the darkness, Carmen Sandiego was off to her next adventure.